THE DEJA VU
CHRONICLES
BOOK FOUR

Cutthroat's
OMEN

A Crimson Dawn

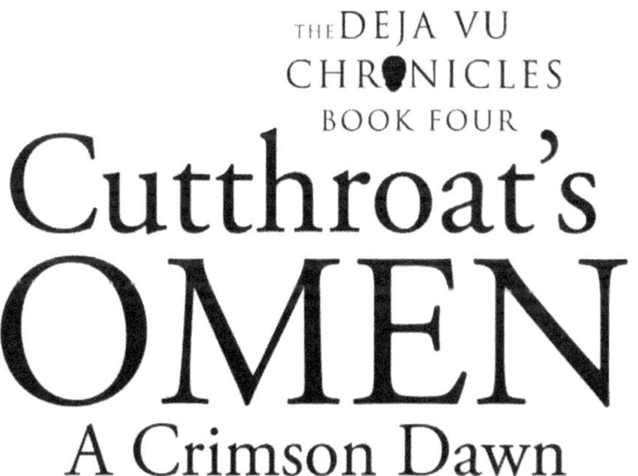

Cutthroat's OMEN

A Crimson Dawn

MARTI MELVILLE

"When it is evening, ye say, It will be fair weather: for the sky is red. And in the morning, It will be foul weather today: for the sky is red and louring."

(Matthew XVI—Wyclif Bible circa 1395)

… and so, it goes forth: "Red sky at morning—sailors take warning."

PART ONE

Infelicitous

One

"AT LEAST HER NECK DIDN'T break when she dropped."

Alex looked askance at Maya, who simply shrugged. "You didn't just say that out loud, Maya, did you?" Alex uttered under her breath.

"Well, it's true and if no one else will say it, I will." Maya folded her arms across her chest in defiance.

The tension in the room had become palpable. Alex bent forward to study the patient's face. Opposite the gurney, a tech was setting up another suture kit and had begun to unwrap the silver-metallic casings over packages of 'No-Burn' ointment, releasing a distinct menthol odor.

"How'd she get these burns?" The questions came from the doctor standing at foot of the gurney. Dr. Paul Jeffries was one of the foremost leading plastic surgeons specializing in trauma injury—his specialty: burns. His unruffled composure did little to hide his rising irritation. "Hmm? Does anyone have any answers?" He took a seat on the rolling stool placed next to the set-up tray.

"Thanks, Dan," Alex said to the young tech as he stepped aside. Alex turned her attention to the physician. "We're not sure, Paul. No one is at this point. I can get Richards in here if you want to discuss the patient with him."

Dr. Jeffries groaned and opened his mouth to object but was interrupted by a rather imposing figure that walked into the room.

"I'm here. What's your thoughts on this, Paul?" Dr. Richards' voice gently deflected the tension felt in the room.

Alex sighed. "Thank you." She was certain there'd be an onslaught of complaints about St. Lukes's lack of tolerance and professional conduct from the plastic surgeon. Fortunately, Dr. Richards had walked in just in time.

"I want to know how she got these burns, but no one has any answers!" Dr. Jeffries snapped.

"No one knows much about the girl, apparently," Dr. Richards responded. "I guess PD is investigating it now. A rather nasty show downtown, I heard." He waited patiently for Dr. Jeffries to answer but got none. "So, what do you think?"

"I think it's a clear case of brutality. She's hung… then burned?" Dr. Jeffries said, and leaned into take a closer look at the charred skin that ran the length of both legs. "And, to make matters worse, it appears there is new injury appearing on undamaged tissue. Clearly these are burns as well," he said, lifting her gown to expose a blistered area above the right knee. "Newly developed within the last few minutes."

"What?" Dr. Richards bent over to examine the patient's thigh.

"I'm telling you, new injury to uninjured tissue, developing from first degree burns, then progressing to full-thickness damage. I cannot keep up with it, and I don't know where the next outbreak will be."

Alex glanced at both doctors at the same time a weight dropped to the pit of her stomach. She fought back the urge to retch.

"Let's call ultrasound—see if we can visualize anything before she goes to radiology. I don't want to exacerbate any of this with radiation through CT," Dr. Richards suggested then added as an afterthought, "although we've already done full AP and lateral pictures."

Dr. Jeffries nodded in agreement then added "Why is she still in these clothes?"

"The fabric is burned into her skin in some places. We wanted you to take a look first before anything was removed." Alex cleared her throat. Dr. Jeffries mumbled something and nodded.

Maya had already picked up the phone and was relaying the orders. She thanked whoever was on the other line, then followed up with, "stat!"

"No one ever says that anymore," she said. "I've always wanted to. Just like in the movies." Alex rolled her eyes and Maya chuckled as she exited the room.

"This isn't the movies. This is a serious problem." Dr. Jeffries began to pace.

Within moments, a tall brunette, with hair that danced against her hips and eyes the color of Chinese jade, strolled in, followed by an ultrasound device mounted on wheels. Brooke's career at St. Luke's was short, but she had big plans. Her free time was spent studying for a clinical counseling. Even now, her charisma was palpable.

"Hi, I'm Brooke. I'm going to take a look with the ultrasound. Sounds good?" She directed her comments to the patient.

There was no response from the woman lying on the gurney, but that made little difference to Brooke, who continued chattering to her patient as if they'd been best friends for years.

Brooke scanned the dark cavities lying beneath blistered skin. On occasion, she'd lift her eyes to the two doctors, peering over her shoulder at the screen. Their interest peaked—apparently the ultrasound hadn't revealed anything of note

"I can't see anything," Dr. Jeffries said, crossing his arms across his starched white jacket. "Do you?"

Dr. Richards shook his head, 'Nah, not really. Just the injury from the noose." The doctors were lost in conversation between themselves, oblivious to anyone else in the room.

Brooke glanced at Alex. The look in her eyes suggested she'd found something—something she didn't want the doctors to notice. Slowly, she slipped her hand underneath the patient, reached into the folds of the fabric not yet burned into the woman's skin. Alex stepped forward. Without warning, Brooke slipped a folded piece of leather into Alex's hand. They exchanged looks as Alex tucked the leather into her pocket.

She glanced again at the patient. This felt preternatural—something neither doctor could fix. Alex shuddered just as Maya entered the room carrying vials and syringes.

Standing silently, at the head of the bed, Rachel monitored the tube snaking down the patient's throat. She glanced at Alex and moved to one side, allowing Alex a better look at the woman's face.

"She looks familiar," Rachel said softly. "I can't place it, but I swear I've seen her before."

"I thought so too." Maya replied. "Back in a sec. I've gotta get more meds."

Chills raised the skin over Alex's forearms as she studied the gentle curves of the woman's cheekbone and ivory skin that had been kissed by the sun on a better day. She knew the face—recognized the woman—but didn't dare voice it.

Lifting one eyelid, Alex peered into a stilled eye of the burned woman. Her pupil stared back, merely a pinpoint from the numerous drugs Maya had been pushing through an IV. Surrounding the woman's pupil, a halo of azure the color of the Caribbean Sea stared blankly at nothing. Alex fought back the gasp that rose from her lungs in a fit of coughing.

"Are you alright?" Rachel asked, placing a gentle hand on Alex's shoulder.

"Yes, I…thank you," Alex said, recovering. "I just need some water."

As she turned to leave, the monitor flickered, and the victim's head lolled to one side. The eyes blinked open, vacant dolls eyes that stared…at Alex. She stumbled backward a few steps, and someone let loose a deep groan from that silent place in the throat meant to hold back curses. There could be no mistake whose likeness the patient bore. Alex gasped and whispered the doppelgänger's name.

"Kathryn."

Two

ICE CREPT ALONG ALEX'S SPINE and, as she reached out to stroke the woman's cheek, she could feel eyes boring into her from behind. She spun on her heels to see the medic standing in the doorway.

"Don't touch her!"

"John," Alex began, but he cut her off.

"No one touches her!" he said, stepping into the room.

"Aren't you supposed to be…where's your partner? Where's your patient?"

He tossed Alex a bitter glare and moved to the edge of the gurney. "I'm supposed to be here."

He lifted the sheet covering the woman's body, allowing his eyes to trace the ligature mark along her throat then drift to the burns along her body. "It starts at her feet and creeps upward." He looked up at Alex, gently replacing the sheet. "She's still burning."

"I know but the doctors think…"

"As a witch."

Alex swallowed. "I know, John. We're trying—"

"The doctors don't know what's happening to her, do they? No one does." He looked at the woman's face as she blinked against tears. "I would have assumed you'd know the truth by now."

"I…Mariel mentioned something, but I didn't understand…I didn't think it would come to this."

"She's burning. You've been heedless of the signs. You could have done something, but you were blinded by your disbelief. It's up to me now. No one else can stop it."

"I don't think—" Alex began but was cut off.

"I was there."

"You?" The hair rose on the back of Alex's neck.

Just then, Maya walked back into the room. Her arms were loaded with IV bags and tubing that she deftly hung from clusters of hooks suspended from a bar in the ceiling. Attached to it was a series of machines that she tapped and poked with one finger, setting the lights to blink.

"How's our patient?" Maya said, forcing a smile. Her eyes darted to the medic. Underneath his shirt she could still see the hint of bandages that wrapped his chest.

"Injured on the job. I was a patient here recently."

"I see." Maya tossed him an *oh, that's too-bad* smile. "And who might you be?"

"There's my man!" The voice was jovial, though tense. "I can't believe you're already working. You know how this goes, man." Mark leaned in and his face lit up with his trademark grin. "This guy! My patient not too long ago!"

"I'm fine," John said. "My place is here."

Alex glanced at Mark and his tone shifted. "Yeah, right. Okay, well, I need to chat with you about something. Let's go somewhere where we can talk in private."

John turned his back and bent over the burned woman. His ear was just inches from her mouth, listening.

Suddenly, the monitor thrummed as the patient's pulse began to pick up its tempo. Maya reached out, ready to grab onto John's arm, but Alex stopped her.

"Wait!" Alex said, nodding to the monitor. Maya froze. "She's been bradycardic this entire time—heart rate in the low 40's. Look..."

All eyes were on the monitor that chirped a steady beat for the first time since the woman had been cut free of the noose.

"She's had runs of arrhythmias. I've had to keep an eye on her because nothing's consistent, and those burns...I can't believe she's still with us," Maya said, and tapped a few more times on the IV pump. "This is nuts!"

The monitor lit up a normal heart rhythm. Mark shook his head. "That doesn't make sense. Look, I really need to talk with you." John continued to ignore him.

"You're the one," Alex whispered. John's gaze lifted momentarily to meet hers. "You're the captain, aren't you?"

He leaned back over the burned woman, this time staring at her face, but he didn't answer. Alex noticed the triton tattooed on his left shoulder and her breath caught in her throat. "I knew it."

"Well, this is a party!" Maya's sarcasm was lost on no one.

"I think the medic needs to be here," Alex said.

"Okay, cool. I'm out." Mark clapped back. "I'll catch you all later when you're not so busy, then." He flashed as smile and turned to leave. "No point in arguing with either of them," he muttered as he strode out of the room. Confrontation wasn't his style and would be unpleasant for them both—something Mark wasn't about to do. Besides, Mark liked John. Whatever was happening, wasn't his business.

"Whoa…look at that! She's in sinus." Maya's eyes grew wide.

A soft whisper escaped the medic's lips. Alex leaned in to hear but could not make them out. It sounded foreign…almost Celtic.

"Are you speaking Gaelic?" she asked.

The medic glanced at Alex and continued to whisper.

"Nice," Maya said, breaking into their conversation. "Her vital signs are normalizing. I guess we've finally got the right mix of drugs on board."

Alex looked at her then back to the medic. This wasn't from drugs—this was something else—something otherworldly and deep.

"John," Alex said. There was no response. "John!" She called out his name a little louder, but once again there was no response. Alex paused and tried one last time. "Captain Phillips!"

He stood and faced her, leveled a frosty glare that bore the weight of centuries pressed down with his gaze. His was an old soul who belonged in a different century…along with the woman.

"You've come for Kathryn," Alex whispered.

A crooked smile crossed his face as eyes glinted. "Ay."

Three

THE SHADOWS CAST FROM THE doorway brought a pensive aura into the room. Alex sensed it immediately and looked up. The figures stood still—granite outlines against the blare of the ER hallway.

"Is it…?"

"Yes," Alex said, her voice trembling.

Without hesitating, the elderly woman glided from the doorway to the gurney. Alex stayed put, almost afraid of what lay under the sheet. John's eyes locked on hers.

"We need to see her," the elderly woman's silky voice was nearly a whisper.

"I'm sorry, but visitors aren't advised at this time… policy, you know," Dr. Richards said. He dropped his hands into his scrub pockets and shrugged.

"These are…" Alex lowered her voice. "This is family. They deserve the right to see her privately, even if it's for just a moment. This is important."

Dr. Richards kept to his casual manner as he looked down at the patient. Tubes threaded from both arms and the ventilator purred below a monitor flashing green and red blips across it. Everything looked stable…for now.

"Please, Dr. Richards," Alex said, interrupting his thoughts. "I'm cautious and a pretty good nurse. I'll keep an eye on her. But these people need a chance to say their last goodbyes."

He nodded and tipped his head toward the doorway. "Let's give the family a few minutes. Alex stays with the patient."

Maya glanced at Alex who nodded.

"Please, everyone out," Alex said a little louder.

"Okay, in your hands then?" Maya said and followed the rest of the medial team out.

Alex looked from the gurney to the elderly women bent over it. John remained where he stood, eyes glued on Kathryn.

"Come in Wendy. She needs you," the elderly Mariel whispered.

Wendy did not move but instead, spoke. "Capt'n?" No one dared speak as the two eyed one another for the first time in centuries.

"Ay," he said. "You're called Wendy now…not Winne or rather, Anne?"

"Yes," Wendy said, stepping inside. "I'm her sister this time around—still family, of course. This is our grandmother, Mariel. You've heard Kathryn speak of her."

The elderly woman turned to face him. Her cool eyes glinted as silver as her hair. John allowed Mariel to study him.

"I can see why she loves you so." Mariel's voice sounded cool.

"But it seems that love isn't enough, now is it… there isn't time for this," John snapped.

"Perhaps." Mariel looked back at Kathryn. "Come here, Wendy. I need you to look ahead, into the past, if you can manage it." Then glancing to Alex, "Did she have anything with her when they found her? A memento or talisman?"

Alex's hand dropped to her pocket. "Only this. The ultrasound tech handed it to me just now, but she wanted it kept secret, appar—"

"Let me see it." Mariel took the leather and gently unfolded it. Inside was another piece, this one thick and elongated with a sharp, black stone at the tip.

Alex gasped. "Is that what I think it is?"

Mariel nodded. "Yes, I'm afraid so. It appears our Kathryn has been busy." She looked at the woman and shook her head.

"And that?" Alex pointed to the thick, meaty sausage piece in the middle.

"Well, obviously, it's a finger, Alex…Get a hold of yourself! We've work to do." Mariel waved at Wendy, who darted to the gurney. She looked at Kathryn's face and struggled to keep the tears at bay. Kathryn's seemed peaceful, almost as if she were waiting for someone to wake her. Still, the ligature mark along her neck appeared more prominent, as did the burns that continued to crawl up her body.

"I…I can't." Wendy let the tears fall. "She's burning and I can't bear to watch it happen."

Mariel sighed. "Then she'll die." Her silky tone had turned frosty. She lifted her eyes to Wendy's. "You are the first and the last—the key to unlock fate."

Alex stepped alongside her, draping an arm across Mariel's shoulders. Wendy began to tremble.

"Perhaps, I—" Alex began but Mariel cut her off.

"Winne was with her too. It is through Winne that we will know where she is." She stared at Wendy who wrapped her arms around her waist, as if to comfort herself.

"What if fate is too horrible? I don't think I can bear it, Mum. Not this time."

"Would you have her die…at your hands, when so many of us are ready to save her?" John began to pace. His tone had turned as hard as his glare, locked onto Wendy. "Would you be the one to let her suffer so and prevent those who truly love her from going to her aid? Are you that heartless?"

The words stung, as did the slap that followed. Wendy lowered her had and John rubbed the side of his face where Wendy had struck him.

"How dare you speak to me thus! I was the one who took her into my arms and nurtured her when you abandoned her for that…that bawdy wretch, Delahaye. I stayed by her side while you recklessly broke her soul."

Loathing danced behind John's eyes. "You know nothing, Anne Bonny!"

"Enough!" Alex's voice boomed. "There is little time for arguing over the past. It's done with! The medical team will return to see what the commotion is about, to be certain. You'd best do whatever you came to do, else get out so that at the very least, I can keep her comfortable while she passes."

Mariel placed a hand over Wendy's and lifted it toward the body. "Help her, Wendy. She needs you to see what we cannot."

"I'll do it for her, but not for you, pirate!" Wendy snapped.

Mariel nodded. She drew strength from the spirits of those who stood with her—and there were many in the room at that moment, most unseen by human eyes. But Alex saw them and allowed her eyes to linger on the empty spaces behind Mariel.

"There are many with us," she whispered into Mariel's ear.

"I know," was all that Mariel replied.

"I'll need to see that map, as well. I was with her when…" He trailed off, watching the women perceive the spirits, dead souls, that he could not. Mariel handed him the leather.

He handled it delicately, studying the markings. "It's not complete. There's more to this."

Alex glanced at him. "And the finger?"

"A memento, methinks. She became rather ruthless in her time, as it were." A half-smile crossed his lips. "Sadly, I think the owner will seek his revenge."

Alex clapped a hand over her mouth. "The ghost! Katherine swore she saw a face on the monitors and a ghost followed her to her car and… She told me it was missing a finger! She knew who it was."

"Ay," John said.

"It terrified her…the ghost that is." Glancing down at Kathryn, she sighed. "Oh Kathryn, if you'd only told me everything."

"Too late now. She's dyin' and ye're doin' nothin' just standin' here, starin' at her." John's brogue had grown thick, along with his annoyance. "I've got to stop this. I must go to her."

As if reading his thoughts, Mariel's glanced at the doorway. "If you go back, Captain…"

He nodded in agreement. "Ay, I know."

Mariel turned back to Alex. "Is Seth….I mean, Brooks where he should be?"

"I sent him just moments ago. He's likely looking for his captain now. You know him as Seth." Alex glanced at John, who nodded again.

"Go," Mariel whispered. "We'll watch over this one. You're needed elsewhere."

"What about her," he said, waving a hand at Wendy, who seemed unaware of anything but the dying Kathryn.

"We'll send her when she's finished," Alex said. John scowled; ready to protest, but Alex silenced him. "As commanding as you may be, Captain Phillips, you cannot do this alone. You will need Winne and my Seth…and our prayers."

He glanced one last time at the gurney. "Ay. Fair warnin'…if anything happens to her…I'll be back."

"You'll be back, anyway. This is a new time and the only way to affect the outcome is through the past." Mariel paused, watching him. "But you haven't much time left. The Omen is strong and she's in its clenches."

He only hesitated a moment longer, glancing at Kathryn on the gurney. "I'm warnin' ye…"

"Go!" Mariel commanded, and John bolted from the room.

Wendy's hand lay over Kathryn's heart, and her other over the crown of her head. The medium's eyes were closed, and Mariel knew that Wendy was far away—in another place, in another time.

Lightning cracked as John rushed through the gaping glass doors of the ER, into the mist, and back in time…back to the 1700s and the pirates' Caribbean.

PART TWO

Moirai

Four

April 1724—the Caribbean Sea

SEA CAPS CRESTED AGAINST SALT-STAINED oak, tossing the ship to one side. The wood creaked against the strain but held tight. Traces of water found its way onboard but had done so through the rails. Of course, that meant the decks were slick and many of the crew would stop amidships momentarily to clutch a line tied tightly against a cleat. Then, as the ship levelled, the same men ran for the next line, hoping to grasp it before the next wave would roll the ship and the slick would wreak havoc again. It was precarious at best, and many novice sailors had been lost at sea on days like this.

One soul stood at the helm, unmoved by the rolling sea and the threat from the sodden deck below her feet. With hands on hips, her pale blue eyes surveyed the men as they scrambled to keep up with their duties. It was a hard existence—this life at sea—but she was accustomed to it now. She had to be.

She was their captain.

"Take the cabin boy to my quarters. I'd like a word with him," Kathryn said to the first mate. She eyed him for a moment, allowing her gaze to travel the length of the man's thigh. "I see you've healed up well enough, Nick."

"Aye, lass…er, Capt'n. That I have." Nicholas touched his brow in salute and made for the brig.

Kathryn watched him—the right-sided limp still evident, though barely noticeable. *He's rather spry for a man who had nearly lost his leg a little more than two years ago,* she thought. She recalled the splintered shrapnel imbedded deep into his thigh. *That was a nasty one, indeed!* Had she not been Chirurgeon when the cannon hit the *Revenge's* stern, Nicholas Scala would not have survived. Most likely, he would have died from Hectic Fever and blood mortification without her skill. She'd done him a tremendous service, and he knew it. She clicked her tongue and wondered if he intended to repay the favor.

"Likely as not," she said aloud to no one. "Pity."

"He's foreign, Kat." Thomas Bourn's tone was sour.

"So are you, Thomas. I've nothing against foreigners, particularly those from Mediterranean waters." She glanced to where Nicholas had been.

"Tame that fire, lass. Ye've a ship to command. Ye'd best keep yer wits about ye, an' stop carpin' o'er your crew."

Kathryn snorted. She glanced around the deck and noticed the creature immediately. Someone had brought a dog aboard the ship—a young one too, maybe only two or three months in age, she guessed. It leapt at a coil of rope, snagging the hemp in its teeth, and shaking its head as if killing a snake. Over and over again, the pup pounced on its prey. Kathryn snickered in spite of herself.

"Maybe the rats will be kept at bay, at least," she said, under her breath.

"Excuse me?" Bourn sounded indignant. "Ye'd best be grateful ye've a crew at all. Men don't take to women as Capt'n, mostly. Though Madame Ching has proved herself a force on Chinese waters, or so I've heard."

No longer able to hold back, Kathryn burst out laughing. "Oh, Thomas. Sometimes you can be so dense." She nodded at the dog and his gaze followed. "I speak of our stowaway."

"Ah, th' dog. Keeps th' rats at bay." He cocked his head and glanced back to Kathryn. "Still, my advice best be heeded. Keep nefarious thoughts to yourself an'—"

"That's a big word, Thomas. Use it wisely."

"Thoughts? Nah…"

"Nefarious." She sneered. "Mind yourself."

He nodded. "—an' a weathered eye on the horizon, Kat. You've a few enemies already an' Wynn's not as quick with th' blade as he used to be, I suspect."

"Wynn's quick enough to guard me when needed. Where he fails, you'll have my back, aye?" She winked at him.

"Aye, sadly, I've me own desires to mind. You're safe, for now, Kat."

Kathryn smiled at him and there was sadness behind her eyes. Whether that was because she could never have him, as the laws of the ship demanded, or whether because she would never choose him, she wasn't sure. Bourn had her heart, to be certain, but her heart wasn't free for him…not just yet.

"Speaking of enemies, let us deal with our prisoners, aye?" She motioned to Gow. "You're still the Bosun, Mister Gow, are you not?"

He nodded. "Aye."

"Methinks, we'd best have a word with those inhabiting in the brig. Please bring them topside, if you would, Bosun."

"Aye, aye!" Gow headed toward the causeway leading below decks. He motioned for the pirate the men had nicknamed "Cap. Seaglass."

"Follow me, mate!"

Cap. Seaglass jumped up from his post on the halyard and rushed after Gow. Seldom did he get selected for prisoner duty. Perhaps today his fate had changed, as well.

Most men stayed to their tasks, but a few wandering looks made their way to Kathryn. Hardly, did anyone expect the young Celtic lass, a kidnapped waif, to rise to Captain the *Revenge*. Never had the ship been dominated by a woman. The mere mention of a female at the helm was unheard of, except in Asian waters. It was evident the men weren't yet used to the change in command. Their looks betrayed their thoughts, but their captain chose to ignore them.

She pulled a piece of hardtack from her pocket and crouched, whistling to the dog. Its ears lifted and the mutt cocked its head before trotting over to her outstretched hand.

"Apparently, ye've made friends with scurvy dogs—all breeds."

The voice came from behind her. She stood and faced a line of men. The simper that crossed her face suggested she cared less what these men thought of her than the dog. Kathryn clicked her tongue and dropped her hands to her hips, the dog waiting patiently at her heels.

"Mister Phillips. I see you've not lost your sense of humor," she replied. "How's life in the brig? Making friends there?"

"I see nothing funny about a healer assuming the capt'n status without merit." His eyes flashed.

"Without merit? Seems I've come about command honorably, not the way you did, pirate."

"That's Capt'n Phillips. The *Revenge* belongs to me, and ye know it, Kathryn."

"You'll address me as your Capt'n!"

His jaw clenched as he glared at her. Kathryn shook her head, knowing he would not relinquish the title, at least not to her. John Phillips had proven to be as stubborn as she. Along with the insistence that he call her "Captain," forcing his respect would only backfire. Besides, the men were watching them, waiting to see who would win the battle of impetuous pigheadedness. Kathryn was determined to be the champion!

"Sails, Ho!"

The call came from the crow's nest, and Kathryn's attention jumped to Dunkin. He pointed to the smaller three-mast vessel leeward. Sure enough, the ship was on approach.

"Schooner. Likely traders from the northern colonies." Scala limped forward as he spoke.

"How do you know?" she responded.

"Seen 'em before."

"In these southern waters? Not likely, Mister Scala." Bourn insisted, and Kathryn thought she noticed the side of his mouth twitch—something that rarely happened except when vexed.

"Hmm…this isn't a battle of acumen, then."

Scala cast her a sideways glance, obviously suddenly lost in translation.

"Means wise," Kathryn responded. "I suspect you're right, Thomas." She glanced at Phillips, who kept an eye on the vessel. "Your interest in this prize has piqued, John Phillips. What do you know that you're not telling us?"

Phillips cleared his throat and motioned to Gow to bring him the captain's spyglass. Gow then looked to Kathryn, who nodded approval. After a moment, Phillips lowered the glass and glanced at her. The sunbaked lines on his forehead hardened as his disposition shifted.

"Mister Scala's correct. The triangular sails bring swift passage for those vessels." He cleared his throat again.

"What is it, John?" Kathryn's tone had changed.

"I've seen those sails before. Methinks her master's familiar, though the capt'n's name escapes me for now." He lifted the spyglass to his eye again.

"You *know* that ship, don't you?" She dropped her hands to her hips and took a stance. "Don't try to hide it, John Phillips. I'll know if you're lying."

"Ay, I know her. I've crossed her before."

Kathryn watched as a hint of remorse touched his voice. She shook her head but kept her thoughts to herself. *He's hiding something…something to surely win the crew's loyalty. This can't be good. I've got to stop him.* "You'd best spill what you're hiding, Phillips, else put us all in danger, you will."

"They'll cross course within th'hour," Cap Seaglass interrupted. "Do we go to arms?"

Phillips met Kathryn's gaze and she thought she saw a slight shake of his head. *He wants us all dead, take back the Revenge without mutiny. Very clever plan, indeed. I'll not have it!*

"Capt'n?" Seaglass interrupted again, and Phillips boldly shook his head, *No!*

"Aye, that we do." Turning to face the crew, she barked the order, "To arms! Ready the guns but hold your fire, on my word!"

Five

WITHIN THE HOUR, THE HORIZON glowed a fiery tangerine, bouncing the last of the sun's light over the water peaks. As if on cue, the current shifted, and so did the schooner's course.

"It cannot outrun the *Revenge*," Scala proclaimed. "She'll try, but she'll fail. Th" *Revenge's* guns be our advantage."

"Aye," a few chimed in.

Phillips stepped closer and was met with Bourn's blade at his throat. "Kathryn don't do this. The man's suffered enough."

"You've grown soft away from your beloved ship, John Phillips. Perhaps you'll learn the ways of the pirate again…if you pay attention." Kathryn waved a hand and Noah Harwood nodded.

Somewhere a low whistle sounded, growing steadily louder and spreading from the bow of the ship where Harwood stood. Whether the oncoming sloop would recognize the signal mattered little, Kathryn intended to scuttle the vessel, take provisions, and leave no trace of either vessel having ever sailed this part of the Caribbean.

"Steady men!" She shouted and lifted the spyglass to one eye. "We fire on my command and not a moment before, savvy?"

The crew replied in tandem. Phillips shifted his weight but Bourn's blade held him fast. "Think on it, mate. I've no qualms 'bout slittin' yer throat, and many reasons to do so."

Phillips glanced from Kathryn to his captor and chuckled. "Good luck with that one. She's a temper to match her wit. Don't think ye'll ever capture her heart, either. I suspect no one will. Indeed, God help the man who does."

Bourn loosened the grip on his blade a bit and stepped back. The words stung. He studied his captive for a moment before voicing his thoughts. "I know ye speak truth, John Phillips, though there's sommat in me gut wantin' to prove ye wrong. Still, it's none o' yer mind what business I intend with Miss Kathryn. We've history."

"As have I, sir." Phillips sighed. "As have I."

Just then, the sea surged and both men lost their footing. Stumbling apart, Phillips took advantage of the break and dashed to the bow, taking Kathryn by the arm. Harwood cocked the hammer of his pistol but did not make eye contact—a clear warning.

"Listen to me, for once in your bloody life, Kathryn, please!"

She glanced at his hand gripping her arm but did not pull away. "Think well, John Phillips—"

"I have," he cut her off. "I'll respect yer post as Capt'n of this ship, provided ye respect the advice of those who've experience where ye've none."

Kathryn shifted her weight. "Let loose of me."

"Not until ye pay heed to advice that will keep us all from getting killed."

She locked eyes with his and felt her pulse pounding. The emerald green of his eyes warmed the frost that iced her heart. "Say your peace, Phillips."

"My name is John."

"Go on, then…John."

He released her arm and glanced at the oncoming sloop. "Ye don't know this Capt'n, Kathryn. I've crossed him before, and while it was an easy take, the crew is cunning and loyal to their commander. In truth, he's a decent man and not deserving of th' ruin ye're about to unleash."

"Get out of my way!"

"Not until I speak my peace."

She stomped her foot and stared at him. "What would you have me to do then, *John*? I've a crew to sustain and that vessel is the means.

"Th' man's a gentleman. He'll do fairly by ye if ye'll just…"

"That the capt'n's a gentleman is not my problem!"

He took a step back and looked hard at her. "What's happened to you, Kathryn? You're not the woman I fell in love with."

She raised her hand and let it fly. Almost immediately, she felt the sting in her palm. The act had little effect on John Phillips, though his cheek showed the mark where she had slapped him.

"Are you finished?" he said, his voice just above a whisper. Kathryn knew that tone and understood that while she may hold the title of "Captain," she did not hold the respect for the position—not with Capt'n Phillips' on board nor with the entire crew, anyway.

"This conversation's for another time…privately held." She turned her attention back to the sloop. "Again, the question, what would you have me do?"

Phillips stared at the vessel for a moment. "Meet me halfway if ye won't listen to reason." He then glanced at the crew in wait behind him. It was obvious the men wanted a prize. He had no idea how long they'd been without plunder and guessed it had been a while, though none of them looked gaunt. Food obviously wasn't scarce, so the salvage would be solely for profit and not survival.

"Halfway or not at all? You leave little to bargain with, Phillips."

"A dangerous situation, indeed," he murmured. "*Listen…to me*, Kat." There was more to that message than words. Kathryn felt it. He had her back after all.

"Beg pardon, sir?" Harwood cocked his head. "What's the order, Capt'n?"

Unsure whether Harwood's query was meant for her or for John Phillips, she stepped up between them. "On my command, Mister Harwood." Glancing at Phillips, she waited for his reply.

A slight grin crossed his lips as he whispered in her ear, "Take ye're aim and fire!"

$$Six$$

"Let 'em know we're here and mean business!"

"Ho!" followed, and Gow sang out, "Shot across the bow!"

The order was repeated and within moments, the cannon erupted. The explosion that followed took out a portion of the smaller sloop's starboard gunwale. The damage was significant, but not enough to sink her. Gow stood at the bow, along with Noah Harwood—any disagreements between them forgotten. Both men waited, watching for the smoke to clear as John Phillips stepped forward.

"She's been damaged but will not founder, methinks." Gow looked to Kathryn for further orders.

"Prepare another volley," she hollered back.

"Aye-aye," Gow responded and darted midships, repeating the order that was soon shouted from several of the men. The powder monkeys immediately began to load the guns.

Phillips reached a hand to her arm, a little more gently this time. "Kathryn, please do not do this. I know this vessel, her capt'n an' crew. We've done them injury enough already."

"Hold!" She shouted, then turned to face him and leveled a dark stare.

"There be better means to take her, and more profitable for yer crew." He paused waiting for it to sink in. "Think on it, Kat. You can accomplish much with the correct approach."

She knew he spoke the truth. Behind her, the sloop shuddered, and the men aboard shouted as they fought to keep her intact. Cries from the injured hung in the air and she swallowed against the lump in her throat.

Your calling is to heal, my Kathryn—the calling of our lineage.

Words whispered in the breeze that suddenly swept from the sloop to the *Revenge*. Along with it, the scent of lavender, the scent belonged to Mariel. This was no accident—Kathryn knew it.

"New orders!" she bellowed at Noah, and to the crew, "Where is Master Nutt?"

"Hoy!" Nutt shouted from midships.

"Take your post, Master Nutt." She motioned to toward the bow.

Nutt rushed forward and took his place at the binnacle. "Headings?"

"Stand by Master Nutt."

He nodded and Cuddy slapped him on the back. The men had resumed their duties onboard, the same duties as when John Phillips was Captain. Things were beginning to shift into place, and it felt right to the men standing there.

Kathryn faced John again. This time she kept her voice low and her emotions in check. "What is it about this ship that holds you so? Tell me all or I swear, I'll sink her."

John's eyes saddened a bit, but only momentarily. "Her capt'n is a man called Minott, William Minott. I know him as Capt'n Minorsat…former capt'n of this vessel ye command."

"The *Revenge?*" Kathryn's gaze darted back to the sloop.

"Ay, the same."

Kathryn sighed. She had not anticipated this. "Well, that's a fine turn of events." Inside, her gut wrenched. *Now, what do I do?* The silent prayer fell on deaf ears. *Ancestors, what would you have me do?* She looked back at John and decided to cast the blame elsewhere. "You could have told me this earlier, John."

"You need to act, Kat. Make a decision before it's too late." John shifted his weight and glanced to the vessel. "You want to be Capt'n…so be one. Do the right thing for yourself an' the crew."

Suddenly, she heard it. A woman's voice whispered in her thoughts: *You know what to do, Kat. This is not our way.* The answer came, clearly, as if the spirit stood nearby. She knew this had been spoken by one of her *stiùireadh spiorad.*

"This man has suffered enough at our—"

"At *your* hands, John Phillips. Not mine."

Not our way…Not the way of the healers…Not the way of the Mellt Sosye.

John Phillips shifted against the weight of the accusation. It was true but hearing it gave new meaning to Captain Minott's demise and John Phillips' contribution to it.

"Ay, he's suffered at my hands. You've now command of his ship—it's yours to do as you will. Don't take all, Kathryn. That's not like you, not your way… at least not the Kathryn that I know best."

Not our way.

She heard the whisper and her consciousness piqued again. Kathryn gasped. "Then you heard it too?"

"I hear men crying out for mercy from their injuries. They need a healer. That is your gift. Not slaughter… not this killing of innocent men." He locked his gaze on hers and knew he'd struck a cord. Though fierce, Kathryn wasn't a killer.

Her breath came hard and another whisper followed: *No coincidences.* The thought burned in her brain, as did his stare. *He didn't hear her whisper…that was for me alone.* She turned from him and issued orders.

"Stand down, men. We collect the prize intact. Take as you please but do not harm the crew. Take the injured below to the sick bay. Then, bring their capt'n to me. I'd like a word with him." Turning to John Phillips, she continued, "You, sir, will join us."

Seven

"Never cross me in front of my crew!" Kathryn paced the length of the cabin, hands clasped behind her back, eyes glaring at John Phillips.

He held her gaze and stood unmovable as she ranted. "Yer makin' a mistake, Kathryn."

"Oh-ho! The pot calls the kettle black."

"Stop!

"I won't stop! You are certainly one to talk of mistakes. Would you like to discuss your foray with Madame Delahaye as the *first* on a long list of *faux pas's* belongin' to you, Capt'n Phillips?"

He chuckled. "Is that what this is about? Yer jealous of Delahaye?"

She stomped her foot. "How dare you accuse *me!* Not jealous, not in the least."

"What then?" He sat and crossed his legs, the way he did when amused. "I can't believe that woman still causes ye to fret so! Ye've got to get over this rage o' yours, lass."

Kathryn pulled her cutlass from its sheath. "Do not use that word with me again, sir!"

"Lass? Fine then, Missy."

The blade sliced the air before Phillips could react. Her blow opened the meaty flesh of his shoulder. He sprung to his feet and countered with his own blade, blocking another attack that surely would have done damage to his other arm.

"Stop this, Kat! I don't want to hurt you, an' ye surely do not wish to kill me."

"Yes, I do!" She lunged.

Phillips gingerly side-stepped the thrust and caught her in an embrace, pinning her arms to her side. She wrestled against his hold, finally dropping her cutlass. Instantly, she called on the Seren but it would not respond.

"Stop…lass. Please stop." His words were temperate, whispered in her ear as soft as a gentle sea breeze. "This rage is not you." He felt her body relax as he caressed her. Lowering his face to her neck, he took in her scent of jasmine and rose water. Softly, he kissed her neck.

Kathryn shuddered and turned to face him. "Stop that!"

He kissed her again. "That's an order not to follow."

"What good am I if I cannot lead a crew? What good are you, if you love another? You see where this rage comes from. I have no purpose…no identity anymore, especially not at sea. Do you even know what you took from me?"

"Not yer temper, that's for certain."

She didn't laugh and instead, wiped her cheek in hope he hadn't seen the tear that settled there. "My identity. That is the one precious thing stolen from me when you kidnapped me, Capt'n Phillips, and I cannot get it back."

She couldn't hold them back any longer and the tears spilled down her cheeks as he lifted her chin and kissed her mouth. For just a moment, she was truly lost, not caring where she stood or what title she held—her only purpose: to love the pirate, Captain Phillips.

He pulled away and looked in her eyes. "You are more than a castaway or capt'n, lass."

"No" was all she could reply.

"It takes no skill to be capt'n of a ship and the crew knows it. Why, any one of those men can command this ship. They don't need you as their capt'n, Kat."

"What then? What good am I when I don't even know myself? What can I bring to this ship and crew, then? If the rumors be true, a vessel be fraught with naught but misfortune, bringin' a woman onboard."

"Healer."

She looked at him, confused for a moment before his meaning sunk in. Kathryn shook her head and paced the length of the cabin. "Ha! Healer indeed."

"You command these men not by shouting orders or bearing a title, any chump can do those things. You command with the power of your abilities and character. Anyone can sail a ship but not everyone can heal." He caught her eye and paused again, allowing his words to hit home.

"Perhaps."

"True, an' ye know it."

"You're a man of tall words, John Phillips."

He shook his head. "Nay, I am a man ill spoken, whose name is dragged through the mud, methinks. Still, I see the truth for what it is, and it is this, Kathryn…men obey you because they need you."

She shot him a look. "No one needs me, and I need no one."

"I highly doubt that. Still, I will tell you that you, indeed, are needed. Think on it. Were you not the one who saved the ship from the pox outbreak? You commanded the men, and they followed you—everyone survived because of you."

"Hmmmm."

"Are you not the soul who saved the life of mutinous wretches—one butchered by meself an' the other keelhauled 'til near death?"

Kathryn sighed. "You make a good argument on my behalf, it appears."

"That is power. The men will keep you safe, guard you if they must, so that you can keep them alive! There is the need, and you wield that power. You alone!"

Pounding sounded on the door. Kathryn jumped. The voices on the other side beckoned the capt'n.

"You've made your point. I suppose you wish me to turn over Captaincy of this vessel to you?" She waited but he did not answer. "I have two conditions before I consider such a proposal."

"I did not propose…"

She turned her back and made for the door. "Upon promise of death, you shall not harm or imprison any of the men who accompanied me to this ship, Bourn and Seth especially."

"Agreed."

"Finally, we shall put the subject to vote."

"Agreed."

The pounding grew louder as she faced her former captain. "We're not finished here. You've much to account for, John Phillips, particularly in regard to your indiscretion with Madame Delahaye." Before he could answer she called out, "Enter."

Eight

MINOTT STARED STRAIGHT AHEAD WITHOUT blinking. His clothes hung loosely about his bones, much like his skin. Notably, he smelled of fish.

"Minott or Minorsat? What do you call yourself, sir?" Kathryn sat on her desk; her leg hung provocatively over the corner edge. He refused to look at her.

"Minorsat is most familiar to those who know me well."

"Well, I do not know you at all, sir. So, perhaps I'll call you Minott. Besides, it has a nice French ring to it." Kathryn studied the man. He remained still as stone though his eyes followed her as she circled him. "You have someone here who seems to remember you, Capt'n Minott."

Minott glanced briefly at John Phillips. "I remember a scallywag and thief by the name of John Phillips."

"That's the one! A scallywag and philanderer, but only a thief, when need be," she quipped.

"It's Capt'n Phillips, now." Phillips took a step forward and Kathryn glared at him. "At least that was once me title."

"I'm the capt'n of this vessel, which I assume you recognize, do you not?" Kathryn stopped and faced Minott.

"Aye."

"Well, therein lies the problem, Capt'n Minott. How to best deal with you and your crew without causing further injury to your vessel." A smile crossed Kathryn's lips. "What say ye?"

Minott sighed. "Injury has already been done. My vessel is small and has suffered much by way of your cannon, madame."

"Capt'n! I would highly recommend ye remember who commands this ship and address her appropriately." The smile had dropped, and Kathryn's scowl returned. She began to pace.

Bourn stepped forward, shifting his gaze from Minott then to Kathryn. She caught sight of his notice and glanced at Minott. His vest was worn but fastened tightly around his frail ribcage. Protruding oddly beneath the wool on one side, a strangely familiar parchment poked through where a pocket-watch should lay. Kathryn immediately noticed the parchment wasn't made of paper. Her eyes widened and she shot another look at Bourn. He nodded but kept quiet.

"Clear the room! Everyone! Out! Except for Mister Bourn. I would have a word in private with Capt'n Minott. You, Thomas, will be our witness to the conversation."

Bourn nodded. Cuddy and two of his mates made for the door. Phillips lagged, waiting, it seemed, for an invitation that never came. Finally, he followed the others and slammed the heavy door shut behind him. When it was clear they were alone, Kathryn stepped up, nose to nose with Minott.

"You have something, there, that I believe belongs to me." She poked his vest where the fabric bulged.

Minott shook his head. "Seems to me, your sights best be kept on the scallywag and philanderer. It seems you've made the good Capt'n Phillips angry."

"I'll not warn you again, Minott! *I* am the capt'n of the *Revenge*. *You* be my prisoner. If you don't plan to hang from the mast, you'd best cooperate and lose your indignant behavior!

He looked directly at her. "As you'd have it then, *Cap-i-tan*. Nay. There's nothing here belonging to anyone aboard this ship." A willful discharge of sarcasm in his voice indicated he did not mean what he said.

"Indeed," Kathryn replied. "We shall see about that." She shot Bourn a look and in less than a breath, Bourn set his blade at Minott's throat.

"What is it you want? My fishing boat? My crew? Those you already have taken or destroyed. Gold? Silver? I have none of that! So, what is left for a sea trollop such as yerself?" Minott spat. Bourn pressed the blade into fisherman's flesh and a thin line of red surfaced. Minott lifted his chin defiantly. "Do it!"

Bourn glanced at Kathryn, who stared out at the fishing vessel. "I will not have my quarters awash in this git's blood. Withdraw Bourn. Take the man topside and tie him to the mast. Perhaps, as his brain bakes in the sun, he'll be more amenable to a conversation without insults."

"Aye, Capt'n," Bourn responded.

"Then…you can hang him or do whatever mischief the crew desires. I have no need of him."

"You're as dark a soul as any pirate, madame!"

Bourn dragged Minott toward the door but not before Kathryn stopped them. Lifting his vest with the tip of her dirk, she exposed the item kept hidden there.

"This…" Kathryn pulled the parchment from its hiding place in Minott's vest, "…stays with me."

Minott spat and Bourn shoved him to the door and up the causeway. When finally alone, Kathryn secured her quarter's door latch then placed the parchment on the table. Cautiously, she unrolled the edges and peered down with pleasure. "It's a diagram!" Fetching her own map, she laid both withered sections side by side, matching the edges where the tattooed strokes broke off.

"Oh Winne! You should see what I have here," she said to no one. "Human flesh, both marked with lines, continuing from one to the other. We were right, you and me. This changes everything!" Kathryn re-rolled both pieces of flesh together and hid them away before bolting up the same passageway used by Bourn and Minott.

"Indeed, this changes everything, including my intentions for my guests and Capt'n John Phillips," she whispered as she pulled the door closed behind her.

Nine

"Divest their little boat of all goods. Leave nothing behind. We'll accommodate Capt'n Minott and his crew back to their carcass of a vessel. Toss the injured overboard—Minott can save his own without our assistance. Indeed, if these be fishermen, they'll not starve!"

Kathryn shouted the orders from the bow. "Aye" came the response from the men, who had set about emptying the schooner. Within minutes, the calm sea broke with the sound of injured fishermen's bodies hitting the water. Several of Minott's crew jumped in after them, struggling to save any miserable life that they could, while others fortified what was left of the smaller ship, and readied to set sail. Capt'n Minott, back aboard his tattered ship, strolled with head held high in spite of his broken spirit. Within minutes, the schooner was set adrift.

"Spoils to the main mast," Gow hollered. The men complied and soon, piles of salted fish, dried vegetables, sugar, aged cheese, and bottles filled with French wine were heaped at its base. "Galley stocked first, next to the stores, last to th' crew."

The men scurried about securing the spoils below ever-darkening skies. Calls from the crow's nest warned of an incoming storm. Kathryn took note and shouted new orders. Her pace slowed only slightly at the sight of a silhouette, just beneath the poop deck causeway. Thunder rumbled and Kathryn brushed off the idea that it could be anything more than an overhead cloud casting shadows. Still, her gut gnawed that something was amiss.

As she took the first step, she heard it.

"You've trouble."

A whisper really. Was it her thoughts nagging or something else? Kathryn shivered. Surely, he couldn't be free of the brig, not yet. Withdrawing her cutlass, she peered around stacked barrels looking for its source. Nothing. Another chill ran along her spine. Someone or something was there…in hiding, waiting for her. "You can wait!" she said, and bounded up the steps, two at a time.

Nutt stood at the binnacle with one hand on the compass. "Mayhaps, we change course nor-norwest. The storm, there, looks angry."

"Aye, agreed." Kathryn nodded. She glanced back at the poop deck but still saw nothing. "Adjust headings as you see fit, Master Nutt. Keep our course to the north. I'd like to see those new world colonies the British brag about so boldly."

"Aye, Capt'n."

Lightning cracked in the distance and the sun faded behind dark clouds. Kathryn noticed the crew had picked up the pace, and someone shouted, "Batten the hatches." *Damn!* The thought of facing foul weather dampened her spirits, especially as she hadn't had time to assess the damages to the *Revenge. She's sturdy but not infallible!*

"Keep to the wheel Master Nutt, and appraise me of any looming setbacks ahead," she said, and lifted her gaze to the skies.

"Aye."

Kathryn's gut twisted again. Something was off. It was time to scan the ship for damage or trouble… the phantom below still clouded her thoughts, with almost greater intensity than the approaching storm. *Now, let's find out who lurks in the shadows.*

With measured steps, she descended the causeway but could see no one. "Who's there? I demand you show yourself!"

Silence.

She took the last stair and turned sharply to face only planking lined with rope that had fallen askew. *Battle did this,* she thought and moved the coiled line aside. "Who's there?"

Nothing.

"This is a waste of my time!" She stated and turned her attention to the activities of the crew. All was in order, from what she could see. Men scurried to tack down anything not secure. *All is well. All is well.* But her gut told her otherwise. Glancing to the forward rails, she caught sight of Seth. *Perhaps he'll know if anything seems off,* she thought. *He's skittish but perceptive..*

Seth watched the water. He paced the bow, but Kathryn ignored it. That was his way, of late—anxious, always eyes on the water as if waiting for something. This day was no different.

"Seth," Kathryn called out to him as she approached. "I need speak with you."

"Not now," came the reply.

"Beg pardon? You speak to your Capt'n in that manner?"

He looked over his shoulder at her, expressionless then turned back to the sea. "Out there…" pointing to the dark cloud that had settled ahead of them.

"What? What is it, Seth?"

"Dunno. Something…"

Kathryn stared hard at the darkness, a sense of dread ran along her backbone and she felt the hair stand up on the back of her neck. "I sense it too. What do you think…?"

"I can't say."

Kathryn glanced back at the helm and saw Nutt give the signal to change course. Gusts of wind pounded against the sail canvases as the *Revenge* shifted along cross currents. Seth took hold of a line for support. *Good call, Seth,* Kathryn thought and did the same. In the distance, lightning flashed.

"We'll be lucky to make it out of here in time," Seth said, a little too composed.

Kathryn's palms tingled. Seth knew nothing about the whispered warning. He'd be no help at all. She glanced at the helm. Nutt held fast to their course, though his brow was creased. *He's nervous.* There was little she could do to calm the men now. They'd surely face a nasty gale, if not a threatening maelstrom. Swallowing hard, she steadied her voice.

"We'll make it," she replied. "Excuse me, Seth. I have business to look after and you have things to do."

Kathryn wound her way to the back of the ship, clutching lines along her way to keep her footing. The sea had turned angry. "Not now!" she muttered under her breath. "Can you not be still for twenty-four hours at least?" As if in response, a whitecap surged and spilled over the rails, blanketing the deck in saltwater. Kathryn hung tightly to the nearest line and waited for it to withdraw back to the sea. "Damn!" was her only reply and she glanced first at the darkened sky then to the water. "You're an angry mistress!"

"You've trouble. It follows ye."

She turned in the direction of the voice but saw nothing. No one was there. "Who are you? Show yourself, ghost. I demand it!"

"Come into the shadows."

Kathryn moved past the mainmast and peered round the galley-way. She heard it—rustling deep in the stocks of supplies kept there. "Come out, mouse! Do not make me ask again!"

"Step a little closer."

"No!" Kathryn stomped her foot and the deck shuddered. Apparently, another wave had hit the hull. "I've work to do and you're a distraction. Speak your peace or hold it. I've no time for games!"

Just then, she saw it and her skin crawled. There had been no wave after all.

Ten

Kathryn felt the familiar tingling in her hands. She glanced down at her palms, both glowing with the familiar blue light. Something pulled her toward the recess where supplies were stored—the boxes and barrels rose as shadows and gave an eerie graveyard feel. This was the place where long-forgotten items dwelt, akin to the bones lost in unmarked graves. Kathryn would not be one of them.

"No more invitations!" Kathryn raised her hands and prepared to strike.

"Wait! Please!" This time the voice sounded timid, weak. Behind it, a figure moved into the light. Tufts of gold curled under a black tricorn.

Kathryn lowered her hands and the light dimmed. "Who are you? You're no member of my crew! How'd you get aboard my ship?"

"I boarded with Capt'n Minott. Fisherman, aye? Now a pirate and a loyal servant to ye, Capt'n." Something sounded off with the voice. It wasn't what she had expected, and certainly not the whisper she'd heard topside.

"You've got real trouble, says I. Real trouble, Capt'n."

"You're not my crew and I'm not your captain…not yet anyway. Trouble, ye say? Prove it or I'll put you to the mast meself!" Kathryn dropped a hand to her hip, fingers tapping the cutlass that she kept there.

"I've heard things…seen things. I 'ave eyes, ye know."

"Come into the light and let me see you." Kathryn moved back to keep distance between herself and the stowaway.

First one boot, and then the other stepped into view. The golden curls bounced as the stranger moved. Kathryn stared hard at the figure and suddenly gasped and drew her cutlass. "A female!" Her voice sounded incredulous! "How did—?"

"Please let me explain…"

Kathryn raised her cutlass to the woman's throat. "You'd better make it swift. I don't take stowaways onboard my vessel."

Blonde curls bounced as she nodded. "Aye…I…I jumped ship when ye overtook us. Some, on me previous ship, raised suspicions and I knew it'd be a matter of time before they'd find out and…well, ye know what sailors do to ladies."

"You're no lady, I can see that. But you're definitely not a fisherman." Kathryn studied the intruder for a moment. "What do they call you?"

"Vane. Charles Vane."

"I highly doubt that. I am familiar with Captain Vane, and you are nothing like the man."

"It's what they call me…the name I go by. What more do ye want, eh?"

"Your birth name."

The stranger cleared her throat. "Charity."

"I see." Kathryn clicked her tongue, and lowered her blade. "Well, madame Charity Vane. I happen to know Charles Vane personally, so don't try lyin' to me again. You're not that scallawag, and you're not a man." She walked a circle around Vane. "What to do with you, aye?"

"Please, Capt'n. Don't let them know. I figured, what with ye being a lady capt'n 'n all, ye'd spare me… give me a place onboard."

Kathryn shook her head. "So, assuming we have no laws against women on board, you thought you'd fit right in and I'd protect you, did you? Ha!" She lifted her chin and laughed. "That's not how things are done here, madame. We have Articles that are followed strictly, even by the capt'n. Stowaways are dealt with severely, as a matter of fact."

Charity dropped to her knees. "Please. Ye know first-hand how it is to survive as a woman at sea. My lot hasn't been easy, but I'm a hard worker and smart…" she tapped her temple with a finger, "…an' I'll earn me keep."

Kathryn sighed and called out to Gow. Then, glancing at Vane one last time, she secured her cutlass in its sheath and turned to greet Gow. "The Articles dictate the laws on board, and my heart's not that soft…

even for a female stowaway. You have no future here, Madame Vane." Kathryn turned and began to walk midship.

"I have information for the *Mellt Sosye!*" Charity called out.

Kathryn stopped in her tracks. "What did you say?"

Just then, Gow appeared around the mizzenmast. "Hoy, Capt'n!"

"Uh, what is the status of the prisoners, Mister Gow?" Kathryn kept her eyes forward and shifted her weight so as to block his view of Charity Vane.

"Prisoners? Capt'n?"

"Aye, Archer, specifically. I've heard tell his apoplexy has worsened. Please check on Mister Archer and inform me of his disposition immediately!"

"Aye, Capt'n," Gow replied and darted away.

Kathryn turned to face Charity. "Now, tell me… what murmurings have you with which to threaten me?"

Charity took a step forward and squared off. Kathryn did the same. This would not end well should they cross blades.

"It's not murmurin's, ma'am. It's ye're calling." Charity swallowed and looked directly at Kathryn. She did not blink for the longest time, then taking a deep breath, stated, "I know who ye be…and I know about the map."

Eleven

"It's cursed."

Kathryn shook her head. "Nonsense. That's your first mistake, lass."

"You want it…badly! I can help you find what ye're looking for." Charity cocked her head, and the two women eyed each other again. "I have the information ye seek."

"Speak plainly, lass, my patience runs thin."

Charity cleared her throat. "I know—"

"You know nothing."

"I know many things…things which ye keep hidden to yerself."

Kathryn laughed again. "Such as?"

"I know the map's made from the skin of witches." Charity smirked and Kathryn flinched. This was not news to Kathryn, but the lack of secrecy was. She needed to put Charity Vane in her place, and quickly.

"Not witches! As I said, you know nothing," Kathryn spat. Fury burned in her veins, rising to flush her cheeks. "Your comments are not enough to save you, Mistress Vane."

"I know enough to keep you interested in sparing me life," Charity said. "Whoever's skin that map's made from, it's got a message that's hidden from ye…and ye want to know what it is. I can help ye there, I can."

"Seems you've caught my attention, Vane. I'm not sure what to do with you exactly, but I won't dispose of ye yet," Kathryn quipped.

There was no sense in arguing with Charity Vane. Kathryn sensed it. The stowaway would have to be made part of the crew, at least until Kathryn could squeeze out the particulars that Charity Vane thought so valuable.

"Aye. I know much about Caribbean witches, I do," Charity responded.

"Obeah. The Caribbean witches ye speak of are known as the Obeah."

Charity shrugged.

Truly the lass has heard of the Obeah! Kathryn swallowed the thought. "The skin comes from the Obeah—witches to those who don't know better." Kathryn sized-up Charity for crew, clicking her tongue in disapproval. "You'll never fool anyone dressed like that. I've got sommat that'll surely hide your figure. We might just be able to fool most of the crew, but you'd best lay low and stay out of anyone's notice," Kathryn said, pulling out her dagger and grabbing hold of Charity's scalp.

Charity closed her eyes and prepared for the worst.

"I'll not slit your throat today, Mistress Vane. However, this must go!" With that, Kathryn sliced off the curls bouncing around Charity's shoulders. "There… ye might just pass for a lad after all."

Kathryn released Charity, who reached for her throat and swallowed hard. "Thank ye, Capt'n." She paused for a moment then added, "I know another secret that might interest you."

Kathryn stomped her foot. "What now? Speak or I'll have your tongue cut out for trying my patience!"

"It's just…Why're ye so angry, Capt'n? What's so threatening to drive ye're temper?" Charity shifted her weight and began to gather the snipped hair from the floor.

Kathryn noticed let out a sigh. "I…I'm not sure, actually." She dropped her voice to nearly a whisper. "Life…people, of that I'm certain. I wasn't meant to be at sea. Not like this, anyway. But I am the Capt'n and ye'd best never forget that lass."

Charity smiled. "Ye're very gifted, ye know. There're those who talk of the *Mellt Sosye* an' her powers to bind the Evil Eye."

Kathryn's gaze snapped to Charity's. "What do you mean…'Evil Eye'?"

A scuffle had broken out mid-ship. Calls for the bosun rang out and the sound of a whip could be heard cracking near the main mast. She didn't need trouble with the crew, not now, not again.

"We'll talk later. Methinks ye're needed elsewhere…
Capt'n." Charity drew out the last, which sounded spurious as she enunciated each syllable.

*Call me a charlatan then. You're the imposter, Vane…
posing as a lad to join the crew.* But the thought only
made Kathryn feel unsettled. There was truth to the
message in Charity's tone…more truth than she
wanted to admit. *Who's really the four-flusher here? The
ship's mate or its Capt'n?*

The commotion at the mast grew louder and
Kathryn glanced toward it. "You'll be my 'cabin boy'.
I'm in need of one. Do your job right and this will stay
between us, savvy?"

"Aye, Capt'n!" Charity smiled again.

With that, Kathryn turned to leave. "Vane…do
not forget you've a skeleton in your closet that's been
exposed. Our conversation isn't over."

"Aye," Charity sang out. "An' you've a calling you've
turned ye're back on." She cleared her throat. "Both will
catch us, in time, aye?"

Twelve

Pssst!

Thomas Bourn looked up from the chirurgeon's instruments spread out in front of him. He glanced in several directions but saw no one. Scanning the repugnant trepan, Bourn shook his head. "Hopeless," he muttered. He'd expected a few hours in the sun would bake off some of the crust stuck on its teeth but so far, the sunlight had failed to disinfect the serrated blade.

Pssst! Thomas.

He looked up again. The surgical devices would have to wait.

Bourn! Here.

Thomas glanced above him and spotted a figure waving frantically from the forward shroud. "Dolt!" Bourn said to himself. "He'll tumble on the next big wave an' someone will have to go in after him. Well, it won't be me!"

Seth waved his arms wildly, and sure enough, nearly lost his hold as an upsurge slapped against the bow, shoving it hard. Bourn stood by, staring up at him, arms crossed, and waited. "Well?"

"I need to tell you something!" Seth said, gingerly descending the shroud.

"Seth, I've got me surgical tools spread out, here." Bourn motioned to the instruments glinting in the sunlight. "I've work to do, lad."

"I know, I know. Don't let me disturb what you're doin'—"

"Already have, mate," Bourn cut in. Seth reached down to pick up the saw. Bourn slapped his hand away. "Don't touch that! It's purifying!"

"Oh, right. Beg yer pardon. Well, then…you see. I have an idea…a plan, as it were."

Bourn bent down to straighten an oversized, curved blade. Its wood handle showed wear and stains turned black from repeated use. Seth grimaced at the sight of it and pointed to a scissor-looking tool that had two blades on either side of a long shaft.

"What is that thing?"

"That's none of your business, that's what it is," Bourn snapped.

"You don't know either." Seth laughed.

"Maybe not, but Capt'n does." Bourn glared at Seth then glanced back at Kathryn. She crouched, huddled in deep conversation with the bosun. Gow still held the "cats" and stood ready to crack it over the back of the next provocateur. Fortunately for the crew, it appeared as if they'd settled whatever misunderstanding had erupted.

"That's exactly what I'm talkin' about. She's in over her head, I tell you."

Bourn locked eyes with Seth. "What do you mean?"

"She's no idea what she's gotten herself into. She can't pull it off. First, she's chirurgeon then she's Capt'n, then some kind of mystic. It's convoluted! We've all been crimped, says I."

Bourn eyed him. Seth still showed the cockiness of a youth and cunning of a pirate, but underneath, he held the wisdom of a man long at sea. His ideas proved to be dangerous at best. Surely, whatever he had in mind would get them all killed.

"I'm in," Bourn said. "What's your plan?"

"In a nutshell, we have to summon the Morrigan."

Bourn shook his head. "Have ye lost yer mind, lad? That witch'll kill us all an' steal our souls before our eyes close."

"Most likely, but it's the only way. Kathryn doesn't know what she's doin'."

"And you do?" Bourn scoffed?

"Not exactly. But mine's a better plan than any she's come up with…or you." Seth stared at Bourn and his look showed determination. "We'll need help."

Bourn shook his head. "No. No. No. There's no one I trust on board. Not even you."

"This isn't something that can be done with just the two of us. I know two gents who're trustworthy—new recruits, as it were, from Minott's crew. They're a bit partial to risk-taking. Perfect for the task."

"What task? I still don't know what yer plan is, except to get us all killed." Bourn tried to read Seth but couldn't.

"We need Kathryn back at her tasks, the ones she does best. She needs to keep her eye on…" Seth motioned to the sky. Bourn could only assume this meant Morrigan or other supernatural beings, he wasn't sure which.

"If Kathryn's the *Mellt Sosye*, as rumored, she would need to keep focused, stay tuned in to…well…" Bourn glanced at the sky and lightning flashed. "It is getting ugly at sea again, all the time really. Mayhaps, the witch is peeved."

"Maybe the Morrigan is hungry for sailors' souls. Maybe she's after us." Seth looked up at the sky and shivered. "You weren't around for the last one. It wasn't pretty. Heads rolled that time…literally!"

"Mayhaps."

Both men glanced from the sky to the sea, uneasy with the way Mother Nature raged. Likely, it was the Morrigan that stirred up the storms, but how two simple pirates could sway the goddess and a healer-turned-pirate captain at the same time seemed tricky—foolish, really.

This would be risky at best, something fit for pirates, and if it meant Kathryn would be out of her own way, and able to finally deal with the angry gods, he could think of no other option. Bourn spat in the palm of one hand and extended it to Seth.

"We have an accord."

Thirteen

Each time Kathryn read the captain's log, her heart pricked…a little bit less these days, but, still, it was painful. The handwriting scrolled intricately across the page belonged to a captain consigned to carpentry topside.

"He deserves it!" Kathryn tried to convince herself, but deep in her gut, she knew he truly belonged to this ship. *He should be the one making these notes, Kathryn, not you! You know it!*

"Stop it!" she shouted and threw the quill across the room. "Leave me alone! I'm Capt'n now!"

The voice in her head would not leave her. She'd heard its chatter incessantly for nearly a week, and she was certain it would drive her mad…eventually.

"Consciousness is nothing but a nasty curse! I don't need you now…never did!" She stood as she spoke to the empty quarters. "Leave me in peace, I tell you!"

Consciousness has saved your life many times over, when you'd listen. Your gut is your compass. You know this. Stop fighting it and surrender into your calling.

"No!"

She threw the logbook at nothing and watched through tears as it skidded across the floorboards. Wiping her cheeks, she lifted her chin in defiance and made her way to face an invisible foe.

Your callousness will be your downfall.

"I will not be ruled by emotions, nor will thought dictate my decisions. This is *my* ship now. I am the capt'n! As such, I will do as I please." She pushed away from the conversation and threw open the cabin's door. As she stepped over the threshold, she heard a faint whisper behind her.

Your downfall…

Your downfall…

Fourteen

"Red skies at night, a sailor's delight…"

"Red skies at morning, a sailor's warning," Seth cut in, absently looking to the water.

The sky was indeed angry and seemed to provoke the sea. Waves rose higher and faster as the *Revenge* moved north. And while the rain had not found them yet, Seth noted several waterspouts in the distance. It was a bad sign.

"We haven't much time. The next ship crossed will be our target." Seth glanced at Bourn for only a moment, to make sure he really was listening, then looked back at the churning ocean. "Not much time at all."

"Well, the sky *was* crimson this morning," Bourn said and grinned, a weak attempt to lighten Seth's mood. It didn't work. "A crimson dawn…the cutthroat's omen. Foreboding indeed."

Every sailor knew the saying. Every pirate knew it's meaning, and it was always foreboding…never good. Most at sea who faced a red sky at morning would meet with foul weather somewhere along their voyage. Add to it the cutthroat's omen and no man (or woman) was safe. It was risky business, venturing out over the deepest waters with both the crimson dawn and the cutthroat's omen.

And the Caribbean boasted of some of the deepest waters in the Seven Seas.

Though men scurried to batten down the ship, the deck appeared empty, void of crew. Kathryn bounded topside and scanned the ship. "Where the hell is everyone? Where's my bosun?"

No one answered.

Lightning cracked in response and Kathryn felt a familiar chill run down her spine. She glanced only momentarily at the blackened sky and shook her head. "Not this day. You will not bedevil my ship this day."

Another lightning bolt knocked her to her knees. Cursing, Kathryn sprang upright then ran in search of her crew…in search of anybody. This day would challenge them all and she was determined the crew would stake a part in whatever lie ahead.

The sails had been dropped and secured. The hatch battened appropriately. It appeared the ship had been fortified in advance of orders. *Good. The men are focused on their duties.* The thought did not ease her angst. She looked astern and noticed Nutt had taken the helm. He struggled with the wheel but did not appear to be distressed about it. Bowed over the binnacle, William Briggs gripped the housing with both hands.

"Is Briggs navigating then? We're sure to be lost," Kathryn muttered, looking at the pirate that had once rowed her in longboat. "This doesn't bode well. I know how poorly you handle a shallop, Mr. Briggs." Thankfully, he hadn't heard her.

She scanned the deck and felt a familiar quake in her stomach. *Something's wrong.* Raising her eyes to stare at the sky, she watched as the clouds twisted on themselves, forming what looked like a face. Holes, where eyes should be, peered down upon the ship— soulless black orbs. *Shark's eyes*, she mused and, as if to confirm her thought, a thin line of jagged teeth appeared and seemed to open slowly. Kathryn heard the hiss of the wind—a warning.

She stared at the holes and squared off. *If it's a battle you want, witch…a battle you shall have!* A wave crashed against the hull, but Kathryn held her footing. *But it shall be on my terms, not yours!*

"Not here. Not now, Morrigan. You shall not take me, my ship or crew this day!"

A hand seized her shoulder. She spun around ready to attack and, instead, stared into blazing emerald eyes.

"Shout at the skies if ye must, but not in front of the men, lass. Not…in front of the crew." John Phillips towered over her, his hand resting on her shoulder in a grip that urged her not to move.

"Release me this instant! The Morrigan. You of all people, Phillips—"

"There's nothing there, Kathryn. Just a storm brewin'. That is all."

"Can't you see it?" She looked up. Nothing. No face. No hiss. Nothing…just storm clouds, as he'd said. She faced him, shaking off his grip, and squared for a new challenge. "I saw her, as clear as I see you standing before me. I saw her."

"No, you didn't. You saw a squall and imagined the rest. You're acting paranoid, Kat and the crew sees it." He nodded to the men.

Kathryn's gaze followed. Scattered around the deck, several men stood, watching her with blank stares. No one spoke. No one moved. "Get back to your duties! That's an order!"

One-by-one, each returned to his tasks, occasionally casting a sideways glance at the lady captain they feared might be cracked. She stomped her foot impatiently, unsure whether it was because of the crew or the pirate who crossed her.

"The men respect me as their captain. They follow my orders and do not question them. I suggest you do the same, Mr. Phillips."

He shook his head. "You only see what you want to see, Kathryn."

"What are you talking about, John? I tell you I saw her face…there, in the clouds."

"Not that."

"Well then, what? You're wasting my time."

"There's talk of mutiny."

She dug in her heels, refusing to let the threat throw her off balance. "They do no such thing!"

"'Tis true, lass. Sadly, you're losing your grip…and their respect along with it. They talk of your waning sanity."

Kathryn spat, and John wiped his face and his eyes saddened. There was little he could do for her, it seemed. And as she walked away, he admitted aloud, "Indeed, she's a pirate…a foul one at that."

Fifteen

Restless seafarers make for maritime misfortunes, so they say.

Most sailors state their intent when boarding a vessel. Gow voiced it best, "I seek freedom, open air, and adventure. It's out there…not to be found on the land."

"Ah, ye fancy Gerbalt then," Captain Phillips replied, impressed that the man knew a bit of the French writer.

"Aye," Gow replied. "He be a sailor, same as you, same as me. We bleed identical salty-dog blood from our veins."

That was enough for Captain Phillips. He invited Gow to join his crew, swear the oath, and assume the rank of Bosun. The offer was accepted, and Gow became a pirate aboard the *Revenge* in that instant. It all happened not too many years ago. So much had changed since then and John Phillips wondered whether the men were the same loyal crew because of it—if not to him, possibly to her. He shook his head knowing better.

Looking around the ship now, it seemed the men subsisted in the tension felt aboard, though many could not reason why. Phillips shifted his stance and considered what might be next for the men, should some decide to mutiny. Reading his thoughts, Gow simply said, "It'll surely end badly for her."

Several men stood at the bow, eyes on the water. They waited for something…in the distance, hidden in fog rising from the ocean's surface. Kathryn snatched a spyglass and peered into distance. She grunted, turned from the rails and headed mid-ship. Hopping onto the capstan, she shouted new orders.

"Take it. Sink it to the depths of the sea. Let them be shark's fodder for all I care." She spat again. "Let it be known that we give no quarters!"

"Aye!" sounded from the few on deck.

"Where be our prize, Capt'n?" Gow said, stepping alongside the capstan.

She pointed across the starboard bow. "There, Mister Gow. If you had eyes to see, you'd see it too. Now, man the guns. We go to battle!"

Voices rose as the men prepared the guns—most were comments about the "Cracked Capt'n" and "Mad as a March hare," or something to that effect. If Kathryn had overheard their comments, she made no show of it. Ascending the forecastle, she again centered the spyglass to one eye. For what seemed too long, she stared at the clouds settled over the sea.

"Naught but a bit o' bad weather, lass." The pirate commented, keeping trained eyes on the water. "Just bad weather."

"And who are you, sir?"

"Pemberton."

Kathryn looked at him. He didn't have the appearance of a seasoned pirate, but then, some of the best brigands appear rather benevolent. "You're not the helmsman who rudely relieved Mary of her duties? What was his name…Earl? Thomas Earl."

"No ma'am. Joseph Pemberton's me name. Respectable, I be. Trustworthy, too."

Kathryn sniggered. "I highly doubt that, sir. You'd be sailin' with the British Navy if it were true."

"The Navy isn't as respectable as one would think."

Kathryn studied him for a moment. This man was different, interesting even. "Well, respectable Mister Pemberton, I trust no one, especially not a pirate I don't recognize. And, as you can see, I'm extremely busy with…"

"It's out there," he interrupted. "My mate sees things the others don't." Pemberton looked around, as if speaking aloud would drum up evil spirits. "He's been called a 'seer'…much like yourself—"

Kathryn's glare silenced him. "I'm Capt'n. Of this ship, in case you aren't familiar. You may refer to me as 'Capt'n' and never speak my name associated with 'seer' again, savvy?" Pemberton nodded and began to withdraw but Kathryn gripped his arm. "Where would I find your mate, Mister Pemberton? I need speak with him."

He glanced down at her hold and pulled free. "Never you mind, Capt'n. I mis-spoke."

She softened her voice to nearly a whisper. "Pemberton, I need his help. If he truly is a seer, as you say, I need his insight, right now. Mine appears to be clouded." She pointed to the sea. "Something's out there. The men don't believe me. Logic says it's a ship, but I've a feeling it's something else."

Pemberton stood his ground. "As I said, I mis-spoke, Capt'n."

Kathryn looked away for a moment. "Please accept my apology, Mister Pemberton. I truly didn't mean to offend. I'm panicked, and that doesn't happen often. Your mate could help me…help us all. Please!"

Pemberton dipped his chin, a signal the conversation was over. "Adieu, miss." But Kathryn wasn't finished with him yet. She reached into her pocket and drew out a few gold coins. Dropping them into his vest pocket, she smiled. "I will pay you more…and your mate…if you'll but help me."

Pemberton nodded and turned on his heel. She noticed, as he fingered the coins that made their way into his breeches, a smile spread across his face, ever so slightly. *The knack of a pirate and a slick fingered thief,* she thought. *He'll return.* She turned her attention back to the water. Then aloud, said, "Ballsy to leave without dismissal, Pemberton." But when she looked back, the man had disappeared.

"Capt'n. Ye're needed at the helm." The shout came from behind. Still, she wasn't distracted.

He'd be an asset, indeed. "Cunning as a fox," she said, and clicked her tongue as she thought of the pirate called Pemberton

Sixteen

As she made her way to the helm, she noticed him…pacing behind the wheel, hands clasped behind his back. The men watched him, too, waiting for orders. "We are alone at sea, Kathryn. Nothing is out there," John Phillips finally said. A look of concern crossed his face though he kept his voice in check.

"That is where you are wrong, Mr. Phillips. I see, but not with these eyes. My sight is not from the physical body—something I thought you understood. Do you not remember I am the *Mellt Sosye*?"

"Are you telling me that you now see things?" The compassion dropped from his voice.

"I am telling you that your physical eyes are not the only way to see. Vision transpires in other ways. Do you not *envision* your objective as a carpenter? See the outcome of your craftmanship before you embark on creating it? And then you do just that—construct a well-crafted table or repair a broken mast? As Captain of this vessel, did you not chart your course from your *vision* of an arrival at some port? You did not see the port, yet you knew it was there."

"Yes, but I followed a map, an outline," he insisted.

"It is no different. I know there is a ship…or something…Norwest off the portside bow. How I know it is no different than how you know an island exists from looking at a silly map," she snapped. "No different, John. It's a *knowing*. It's in my gut. You have felt that same *knowing*. I've watched you use it in the past."

"Mayhaps, but I trust what I see with my eyes," he replied.

Kathryn grunted and shook her head, eyes focused on a knot in the deck's planking. "Pity you do not trust that gut-feeling now. Perhaps you would find yourself in different circumstances." She turned on her heel and shouted orders to Gow. "Prepare for battle."

Gow stared, lost in thought for a moment, then traded looks with Briggs, who scratched his head and shrugged. A weak reply followed, "Aye." The order was relayed, and the men moved into position. Whispering objections between them, most just nodded and gestured.

"Nothin's out there. None a-tal!"

Kathryn jerked her attention toward the commentor but failed to find the orator. In that moment, the wind hummed.

Seventeen

"Are you sure about this?" Seth took a step back and studied the contraption.

"Of course! It'll work. Trust me, mate!" Girgl Walters stood taller than most believed, given his aptitude for sporting. Most lanky sailors moved awkwardly, but Girgl's agility and smarts made him the exception. Everyone liked the man. Most everyone trusted him, too. He adjusted a large drill attached on the top of the contraption and smiled at Seth. "Drebbel's man showed me."

"Who's Drebbel?"

Girgl stood upright and stared at him. "You mean to say, ye never heard of Drebbel? Cornelius Drebbel, the Dutchman?" Dobs and Seth both shook their head. "The two o' ye both best get educated!"

Blank stares and a shrugged shoulder in response. "Dunno what yer talkin' about, mate."

"Drebbel is famous for his diving boat. *Under water*! It dove into this very sea a full fifteen feet!"

"With someone inside?" Dobs shook his head in disbelief.

"Aye!" Girgl patted the side of his creation. "Modeled after the original submersible."

"And you're sure this will work?" Seth touched the greased leather tacked along the seam that secured several barrels, one on top of the other. The whole of it looked like an oversized potato.

"And three is all you need to run it?"

"Aye! Pedro, me, Seth, and ye. 'Course, I'll be on th' outside, sendin' off the finest crew ever to sail the deep blue sea…" Girgl elbowed Dobs' ribs. "…if ye get me meaning." Girgl let out a bellow and wiped the tears from his eyes. No one else laughed. "It be a good joke. Yer all yellow-bellied, that's all."

"Course we're yellow. Seth an' me don't fancy dying in that contraption. Not today, anyway."

"Ye won't be dyin', mate. Ye'll be securin' our fortunes. The plan's set in stone, an' once Capt'n Kathryn finds out 'bout it, she'll back the idea, herself!" Girgl nodded and re-adjusted the drill, just for show.

"It'll never work!" Dobs stated.

Seth glanced at him then looked back to the contraption. "What's left to do then? When do we set off in this thing?" He walked a slow circle around the submersible, apparently inspecting Girgl's handiwork and occasionally patting the thing just to be sure it was sound.

"I've just the finishing touches to put on." Girgl paused and clapped his hands. "Oh-ho! And here it is now."

Thaddeus and Pedro approached, each carrying two buckets filled with steaming pitch. The stench reminded Seth of the boatyards back in his village. He stepped back but could not escape the smell.

"Where yo wan' dis?" Pedro asked, setting the buckets down where he stood, eyeing the dive boat.

"There is just fine! My thanks, mate," Girgl responded. "Just fine indeed. We must hurry men, before it cools. Cover the whole of it but make the seal especially thick at the joints." He pointed to the leather tacking the barrels together.

"It'll sink," Dobs interjected. Thaddeus nodded but no one else paid attention to Dobs.

"This's a bad idea, Girgl. Bad idea, indeed" Thaddeus stated, setting his haul next to the dive boat.

"It's a brilliant idea," Seth piped in. Pedro shot him a dark look, but Seth brushed it off. "We take this submersible vessel to sea, pitch it below the surface of the water so as not to be detected, and dive below whatever's out there…a ship preferably. Then, usin' this drill, we scuttle her from beneath. She'll take a pretty minute to sink, allowin' our mates time to overtake the crew and plunder before the entire ship is lost."

"What happens to you…in that thing? Once the fightin' starts and cannons fire, ye're likely to be obliterated yerself," Thaddeus asked.

"Ah, now. That's the beauty o' it," Seth replied. "We'll already be back onboard the *Revenge* when their crew discovers they've been hit and their hull's filling with water. The distraction will make for an easy plunder. Likely, no cannon will be needed."

The men stared at the contraption, lost in thought, and appeared to ponder the well-hatched plan Seth had just laid. Most likely, they were considering who would be the unlucky bloke to crawl inside it first.

"Has it been tried? Tested out, as it were?" Thaddeus asked.

Girgl shot him a look and shook his head. "Ye just brought the pitch, mate. How'd we test it without pitch?" Thaddeus' blank stare forced another response from Girgl. "Course not, mate. Its maiden voyage be in the offing, forthwith…when the pitch be set."

Pedro held his hand above the top of the dive boat and repeated Seth's nickname for it. "Submersible craft. I like dis idea, but I won' get in dat ting. Man's not made to swim wit' da fishes, unless he be dead."

Steam rose from the submersible, its black tar bath setting in slowly. No one on board the *Revenge* noticed the smell of hot pitch, apparently, because nothing was ever said of it. Some tell that Seth paid off the tongue-wagglers with doubloons from the cash kept deep within the captain's quarters. None of the other pirates knew of the treasure, not even Kathryn. But John Phillips did, and he and Seth had kept close company in recent days.

"Death trap, says I," Pedro shook his head as he spoke. "Dis feels o' dark mojo, if ye ask me."

"No one asked you, Pedro," Girgl replied.

"It's just his superstitious nature goin' all wonky on him again, mates." Seth patted Pedro's shoulder. "It'll be fine! An adventure, Pedro! Think of it like that."

"I'll not be in it. Not me," Pedro insisted. "Th' weather's not to our favor."

Seth waved a hand. "Don't be a yellow-belly, Pedro! Weather's above the water. We're going below."

Pedro shook his head. There'd be no convincing him otherwise.

"Well then, we'll just have to find another bloke to join our little crew, won't we." Seth glanced at Dobs who swallowed hard. "You, Dobs…me…and I know of one other we can get in place of Pedro. Trust me."

All eyes stayed glued to the submersible, none looked trusting…all appeared wide and fearful.

A breeze rolled across the deck and chills crept along the spines of those onboard who recognized the signs: portents that signaled the pirate's legends filled with all manner of symbology and warnings.

Songs were sung of the demons of the deep. Tall tales spoke of nefarious sea creatures. All of the stories spoke of impending doom, something most seafarers were familiar with, especially in the Caribbean.

Overhead, the moon shifted from behind the clouds—a bad Cutthroat's Omen born. It was then—Kathryn screamed.

Eighteen

Wind at sea sings differently. It drives the currents, lifting them into waves that dash its song underwater. Sea creatures hear it. So do seasoned sailors.

Those with trained ears can hear the wind in dissonance. Some call it the 'Siren's Song' and blame the mermaids. But to those who have sailed the seas long enough, a dissonant wind is something to be feared.

At the moment, over the Caribbean Sea, the dissonance was deafening—a wind song the likes of which most had only heard about in rumors. But he'd heard it. The look he gave Pemberton said it all. Neither Danny nor Pemberton wanted to voice their fears aloud. Finally, after several minutes of listening in silence, Danny spoke up. "Not like any t'others I've heard. This one's differ'nt."

"How so?" Pemberton asked, though he really didn't want an answer.

Danny explained pitch and tone and wind factoring the strength of waves. Pemberton nodded politely, eyes glazing over a bit.

"Okay, but how's this one peculiar?" Pemberton pressed again. Maybe more distinct verbiage would trigger details. "Why's it so unusual?"

Danny paused and looked at his partner for a moment. Frightening poor Pemberton would be bad for them both…but so would ignorance. Danny sighed. "Because it's a witch's wail," he finally explained. Pemberton shrugged, so Danny continued. "The wind's guided by a witch's breath. It's happened only once… maybe twice before…according to legends. Ye've heard of tales, when the Loreley sang, dashing the ships against those rocks in Germany. No one survived. The second, with the Sirens song. Same thing happened, and those ships were doomed too. Germans call 'em 'Nixes' but Welshmen know their real name's 'Morgan'."

"Like, Morrigan that Capt'n Kathryn keeps yappin' about?"

The men stared at one another. Again, the silence screamed thoughts neither wanted said aloud. Pemberton glanced at Kathryn, then back to Danny. "You perceive what we're all knowin'."

"Yes," came the reply. "I heard it too, when she screamed at the clouds."

Pemberton nodded. "Morrigan. She said the name."

"That's the same Morgan we're talkin' about, aye. One and the same."

Pemberton hung his head. "She's Scots' blood in 'er, and John Phillips is Welsh. He'll know." He looked at Danny with pleading eyes.

"Aye. They'll both know soon enough."

Nineteen

KATHRYN HAD STOPPED SCREAMING, BUT she couldn't avert her eyes. In fact, she didn't blink. *A trance* someone said. *Transfixion* said another when he really meant *spell*. Everyone on board could see that Kathryn was, indeed, transfixed and in a state that only those rightly known as "Seer" would understand.

Danny recognized the symptoms. He stayed hidden behind the capstan as he watched her, his eyes darting from Kathryn to sky and back again.

"See that?" Danny whispered. "Jumbie's got 'er."

"What's 'Jumbie'?" Pemberton's face drained of color. "Sounds bad…very bad, indeed."

"Obeah spell-binder got her. Black magic. The Jumbie locked eyes wit' her." Danny scanned the ship. "We need to find Pedro."

Crossways, Charity also kept an eye on Captain Kathryn. A chill ran down Charity Vane's back, and while she couldn't see what had captured Kathryn's attention, she sensed it was bad. The chill stung her again and again, forcing Charity to move. She caught sight of Danny and Pemberton, and sensed they felt uneasy too. Quickly crossing the deck, ill-hidden by the bulk of the capstan, she crouched alongside the men.

"What is it? What's wrong with her?" Charity asked, her eyes never leaving Kathryn.

"Obeah-fiyo. Where's Pedro?" Danny asked. Charity nodded to portside where Pedro stood. "Fetch him an' bring 'im to us. Don't let anyone see you."

"What am I? Ye're bondsman?" she snapped.

"Yer no bloke an' not bonded to anyone, methinks. So, quit yer fussin' and go! We've no time to lose wit' this." Pemberton piped in.

Charity *harrumphed* and marched to where Seth was hunched in deep debate with Bourn and Pedro. He stated they were "…discussing important things" and not to bother them. But Charity whispered something that made Pedro jump. He followed her and moments later, huddled in the cover of the capstan along with the others. Glancing behind, she caught sight of Bourn fasten something around Seth's ribcage.

"What're they up to?" she asked Pedro.

"Dealings o' their own an' best no be disturbed." He gave her a warning look. "It's none o' our business, aye?"

She nodded but her gut told her something was amiss. By the time they reached Danny and Pemberton, she couldn't hold back any longer. "Something's going on with this ship…this crew. I've got a bad feeling about this."

"It *is* bad, Charity. I've seen it before. We've got to do somethin' 'fore her shadow gets snatched," Danny said, then lowered his voice. "I saw it too. The Jumbie's face. It's up there watchin' us. But don't look at it else it'll snatch us too."

Pedro's eyes widened. "Dis be dark magic. If it truly be Obeah dat sent a Jumbie, Capt'n Kat'ryn's be marked wit' *maljeau*. It might be too late."

"But you know what to do, Pedro. Ye're from th' Islands." It was more of a question than statement, and Charity wasn't sure she really wanted the answer.

"I know she be in trouble. I know dis only be fixed by Obeah. Da capt'n need a bush doctor. Only Obeah can fix her."

No one spoke for a moment. Glancing at the helm, Danny noticed that Nutt still held the wheel. "We're in trouble mates."

A deep baritone responded, and the little assembly startled. "What's with all the whispering, mates? You're not discussing things that could possibly earn ye time in the brig, now are ye?" Bourn smiled broadly, but that soon disappeared when he caught Pedro's eye. "What's wrong? What's goin' on?"

"Obey-fiyo shadow-bound da capt'n. She's marked wit a maljeau. Look at her…"

Bourn glanced from Pedro to Kathryn. "This changes things." His face blanched as he watched her stone-still staring at the black clouds. Rain had begun to fall and still she did not blink…only staring, fixed on an unseen visage in the darkness. "What can be done, Pedro?"

"She needs a bush doctor," Charity piped in. "She needs go to an Obeah priest…what he said." She pointed at Pedro.

Bourn thought for a moment, then glanced at the helm. "No one can know. We'll have to convince Nutt to steer the ship to shore. Find a bush doctor there."

"We can't do that!" Pemberton's voice rose a little too loud.

"Quiet, Joe! You'll only roust the others, and we need to keep this between us." Danny snapped.

"Why? Why not?" Bourn asked.

"Because of him…" Danny pointed to a figure standing at the rails. His silhouette strong and commanding, the stance of an experienced pirate captain.

Twenty

"I'll do it. I'll talk to him. Much as I hate to admit it, we need Capt'n Phillips back in command." Bourn shook his head as he made way to where John Phillips stood at the rails, muttering under his breath, "She'll never forgive me for this one." John Phillips appeared lost in thought as he stared out to sea. His deportment was that of a sea captain, a testament to Bourn of what should be the man's position. "Ye're doing what's right, Bourn. Steady now," Bourn said to himself as he approached.

"I know why ye seek me out, Mister Bourn," Phillips said without turning to look. "I cannot help ye."

Bourn sighed. "Listen, Phillips." The indignant address caught John's attention. "This isn't easy for me…not for anyone on board, but I've an interest in Kathryn's well-being, as much as ye."

Phillips spun around and fire blazed behind his eyes. "Ye know nothing of the sort. Although, I've no doubt ye're interest in this ship's cap'n lies well beyond *her* well-being. It's yer own interests that keep ye trained on Kathryn, and I ought to run ye though because of it!"

Bourn took a step back. He glanced at Phillips hand resting on the hilt of his sword. "There's where you error. I need to explain what happened on the island. How I came to be in Kathryn's company."

"Go on. But I warn ye…" Phillips turned back to the raging sea. "You've not much time so make it quick."

Bourn looked at the water and noted the black clouds overhead. He would have to make this a very short story, indeed. "I was given th' task to take Kathryn to sea, in a jollyboat, no less. When the time was right, I was to dispatch her overboard an' leave her to the sharks. I couldn't do it." Bourn hung his head and sighed. "She…she…"

"Go on."

"Her intent was only to get back to the *Revenge*… to get back to you."

Phillips looked at Bourn. "How do ye know this?"

"Because she told me as much. I knew I could never have her as my own, and I wasn't willing to take her, although I had plenty o' opportunity. But that's not the man I am. My intentions be honorable, though I've had my share of fair ladies, and some not as willing as others."

Phillips stared at Bourn for a moment. "Then why not Kathryn?"

"I cared for her. I guess that's most o' it. But there's something else about her. She's meant for somethin'… somethin' I'm not able to be part of, methinks."

"Do you love her?" Phillips' eyes locked on Bourn's. The men stared at one another, neither speaking. Finally, Phillips dropped his gaze and sighed. "I do not hold you at fault. She is unique, and in spite of her many faults, it's impossible not to love her."

Bourn said nothing.

"You know there will be a time when you must turn from her. Choose the sea, man. I do not wish to kill you should we be forced to duel."

Shaking his head, Bourn simply whispered, "Neither do I."

They stared at the sea, side-by-side standing at the rails, both in love with the same woman. But there was no question as to which man held Kathryn's heart.

"She loves you. She will always choose you. I'm just a sailor given the task to row fare in a jolly boat. That's how she sees me. Ye, sir, be Capt'n of the great vessel, *Revenge*—and ye both love her most.

Bourn spoke the truth, and it had earned John Phillips' respect. Kathryn had put them both in a difficult position, but it wasn't her fault. She was who she was, and men could only fear her or love her. They each had chosen the latter.

"I do not wish to be yer enemy, Mister Bourn. Ye're good with a blade an' the men seem to like ye. Still, I don't trust you," Phillips said.

"And I don't trust ye, either."

"Then we seem to be at an impasse."

Bourn nodded in agreement. "What now, John Phillips?"

Phillips stared at the water for a moment before speaking. "I will take care of Kathryn, but I'll need yer help."

"Aye! That I can do, Phillips." Bourn breathed a little easier. "What else?"

A smile lifted one corner of Phillips' mouth as he considered Bourn's question. "I take back me ship!"

Twenty-One

OVERHEAD, THE CLOUDS DARKENED, FILLED with streaks the color of blood and black bile—violent and ill. Lightning flashed again and again, in hues of bleached bone that bespoke of ethereal beings hiding within the haze. There was no question that this was no ordinary storm.

"Maelstrom!" Dunkin shouted from the crow's nest.

An orchestrated chorus of sea and sky crescendoed into a surge of blues, as cobalt-charged fluxes rose into a climax of thunder and electricity. The whirlwind cast a magnetic torrent that fanned out to the ship—its entirety enveloped in a blue electric current that caused the *Revenge* to quake. It all appeared to be centered around Kathryn.

The current seemed to recognize her, and suddenly pricked her consciousness. At that moment, even Kathryn recognized the danger they were in, should they remain at sea. She blinked for the first time in hours and scanned the deck for her crew. "Gow!" she cried out, but he was nowhere to be seen. "Bourn!

Where are you? Anybody!" Kathryn stumbled forward and clutched the rails, staring directly into the electric funnel. It didn't take long for her to realize the best course would be to make harbor somewhere and wait out the storm.

"Where are we?" Kathryn snapped. "Headings?"

Nutt had taken the wheel, his face flushed. "Capt'n, I know maps. I know our course. What I don't know is how to sail this ship."

Kathryn shot him a look. "I agree. So, again, Master Nutt, in god's name…where are we?"

Lightning cracked overhead—a sound like glass breaking somewhere in the sky. Kathryn glanced at it then back to Nutt.

"I would need to consult the charts to be certain, but I believe we may be somewhere near the Antillas Mayores."

Kathryn stomped her foot. "Give the wheel to someone who can steer this vessel and go consult your confounded charts! I need our bearings."

Nutt motioned to Tate. He nodded and strode to take the helm. But before he could reach the wheel, Danny knocked him aside and took hold. To be certain, his fist clenched in preparation for a fight, but Nutt intervened. "I know what they're doin', Tate. Let him be, for now. Stand ready, but let the bloke take the wheel…for now, as I said."

Tate growled but backed away and Danny stood fast, steering the ship for land. Kathryn noticed the scuffle but cared less. Her mind elsewhere, she looked at the sky again. Water rained down from the cloud cover, slicing the air in torrents, and stinging her skin. This was no typical Caribbean storm. No—something evil permeated the clouds and Kathryn knew it sought her out.

"This isn't going to end gently, is it?" Bourn whispered.

Kathryn jumped, not realizing he had crept up from behind. "No…no it's not. There is an entity in the storm. You wouldn't understand, though, would you, Thomas?" She turned to face him; strands of sopping hair dragging over her eyes as the rain dashed her face. "Do you also believe I'm cracked?"

Bourn just stared at her.

"Apparently so. It seems I run solo in this mad dash to save our lives and the ship," she replied.

He shook his head. "I don't think you're crazy, but I do think ye'd best get yer wits about ye because the rest of the crew does."

"I don't care what the crew—"

"Ye'd best reconsider. The men will be yer greatest ally or fiercest foe. I've seen what an angry crew can do, and ye're headed that way, Kathryn."

She glanced at the sea then back to him. "Are you my ally, Thomas? Am I assured you have my interest at heart…a loyal friend, as it were?"

Bourn nodded. "You know that I am. You've always had my heart, Kathryn. From the moment I first laid eyes on ye, I fell into a spell, captured by yer fiery spirit. I've loved you since the moment we met."

"And I love you, Thomas, but not in the way you would have it. My heart's gone cold. All I have left are my acquaintances. That's all that I need from you, now."

"Friends? Mates? That's all?" Bourn stepped back and took her in. "I told him ye could never love anyone, least of all him! Least of all me. I told him, I did. Only the ship. Only the *Revenge*."

"Who? Who did you tell, Thomas?" She grasped his shoulders and was about to shake, but caught his eyes wander to the rails where John Phillips stood. "You told Phillips these things? Damn you, Thomas Bourn! You know nothing…nothing at all!"

She released him and began to pace. The blue current followed her with energy that increased its intensity along with her anger. Bourn noticed but refused to back down.

"Ye can damn me to the depths. Hate me yer entire life, if needs be. But I'll never turn from ye as ye've turned from me. Yer heart may be calloused and cold, and yer blood run black as tar, but mine will never be so. I'll have yer back, even when ye don't deserve it, Kathryn."

Bourn kissed her cheek and turned to leave.

"Thomas…"

He paused and looked at her.

"If that be the case, I have one request of you."

"Anything," he replied, and wiped his eyes. Kathryn couldn't tell if it was from the rain or a broken heart. "What do you want me to do?"

She stepped closer to him and pulled him in. "It's regarding Seth…" she whispered.

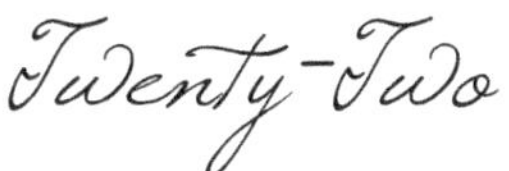

DARKNESS WAS PALPABLE INSIDE THE brig. Though the cage had been made of iron bars intended to let in whatever light filtered from the cracks in the deck above, only the night sifted through. Pitch black…the color of tar used to fill gaps and seal planks. It was in this obscurity that eyes, without sight in the daylight, held visions.

There, in the pitch blackness of the brig, Archer found sight.

"What are ye?"

"I am Balor."

"What do ye want with me?" For the first time, Archer shivered in the brig's biting cold.

"You recognized the threat of what she was. You tried to stop her. From the beginning, you tried to stop her."

"The capt'n?"

Balor said nothing but stared with yellow eyes at Archer. He shivered again.

"Ye're right on that, mate. Th' wench be naught but a scally. She's no capt'n to me!" Archer spat and steam rose from where it landed.

"You've much to do still. You know what it is…what lies before ye."

"Aye. That I do. That I do." He paused, scratched his head and brushed off the clumps of hair that stuck in a grimy fingernail. "Ye've not addressed ye're purpose here, Balor. Whatever ye be, ye're foul and stink of death."

Balor's lips twitched and Archer noticed teeth that weren't human. *"My purpose is to prepare the way. She's here and ready to claim the souls."*

"Ye speak in riddles, mate. I've no idea what ye're talkin' about but…" Archer fingered the bars on his cage. "…but if ye let me out of this crate, I'll be of use to ye. Ye have me word."

Balor studied the pirate for a moment. *"Should I grant your wits and your freedom, you'll pay outlay. Nothing comes to mortal man without heavy expense to his soul."*

"Name your price, demon."

"You stay under bondage…but to me…to her. Do you understand?"

Archer spat again and moved back, deeper into the cage. "Never! I'll never be in accord with that wench!

She's a pox to us all, 'specially Capt'n Phillips. She's bewitched him, took o're the ship, an' hexed me by th' Obeahfyo. She's up to somthin', I tell ye. She's a map that leads to…to…treasure most likely! She…"

"*Silence!*" Balor's voice was but a whisper but the bars that held Archer rattled as if cannon fire had just discharged. Archer shrank back into the shadows. "*I speak not of the Mellt Sosye, fool! I speak of the Morrigan. She awaits and requires ye're soul.*"

"I've decided, my soul isn't for sale."

Balor turned away. "*That is of your choosing. Your wits shall be withdrawn, and your freedom lost, as you wish.*"

"Wait!" Archer shouted. "What do you require of me?"

"*Your loyalty to the goddess, the Morrigan. Dispatch the Mellt Sosye and send the crew's souls to the goddess.*"

"Kill the wench?" Archer chuckled and moved into a shaft of light. "Why didn't ye say so in the first place? I'll gladly 'dispatch' the wench! That goddess of yourn can have whatever she wants. Th' deal is this—my mind stays keen and these bars…" He waved his arms at the cage. Balor walked to the staircase. As he moved, the bars crumbled, and Archer was freed. "One more question, Balor. What of ye?"

"*I meet with the Mellt Sosye. She has yet to learn of me.*"

Twenty-Three

"It's on the ship! I saw it…spoke to it! Somebody…" Kathryn screamed as she bolted up the causeway. "Somebody's seen it. Where…?"

Bourn clutched her arm. "Who? Whos's been on the ship, Kat?"

"Balor! It's not a 'who,' it's a phantom, a demon! Spoke to me…waited for me in my quarters, then threatened me…threatened the ship." She broke free of his hold and ran to the bow. The electric current had turned a deep shade of violet, swirls of black lifted skyward as she panicked. "We've got to find it."

Bourn followed her, glancing at Phillips, who joined the chase. Overhead, the sky cracked in crimson streaks that lit up the sky. Kathryn ducked and looked overhead.

"Perhaps there. It hides with the Morrigan, to do her bidding." She raised a fist. "Damn you, Morrigan and your ilk. You'll never take possession of this ship or my crew. I'll damn you to hell myself before that day!"

Another lightning bolt hit the water just ahead of where Kathryn stood. The water hissed in anger and steam covered the deck. As if responding to a master's bidding, the cerulean current lifted from Kathryn and joined the sky in a brilliant kaleidoscope of pitch, crimson, and sea speat. All of the elements combined—a perfect blend of earth, wind, and water. The only element missing belonged to the *Mellt Sosye*. And she would not deliver.

Again, a fiery bolt hit the sea, illuminating the darkened sky and showering the *Revenge* in sea water. The hiss that followed this time sounded beastly—a guttural *hiss* the men had heard before.

"Not again!" one of the crew cried out.

"Take cover!" another shouted, and the crew suddenly scattered.

John Phillips stepped up to the foremast. "Keep to yer posts! Abandon now an' ye'll face the cats. Yellow-bellied dogs...all o' ye!"

At the sound of his voice the men snapped to. That tone and authority only came from their true captain, or so they believed. This was an order they knew best to keep. Kathryn barely noticed but Bourn did. He stared at the Captain Phillips for a moment, touched his brow, then pushed forward to where Kathryn ranted.

Bourn took hold of her arm. "Kathryn...come with me." She looked at him with black eyes. "Kat!" he repeated, but she held fast.

"Allow me," Charity stepped up and Bourn released Kathryn. Charity then took her by the arm and spoke, nearly a whisper. "Lass, come with me."

Kathryn allowed herself to be led away. "Balor," was all she said.

In that instant, the bow exploded in fire and charred splinters, projectiles that rained down upon the entire ship. "Fire" someone shouted, and several men rushed to put out the flames.

From the helm, John Phillips commanded the men. "Hard to starboard. Now, Mister…" He paused. "For godsake, who's at the helm? Mister Gow, locate Harwood, if you would and bring him to the helm."

"Aye, Capt'n." Gow disappeared below deck.

"You, there!" Phillips shouted at the man steering the ship. "You will remain at the wheel until relieved, shortly."

"Aye, sir," Danny called out.

"Meet her then hold course thirty degrees west to landfall. Nutt? Course?"

"Twenty-six degrees north by seventy-three west." Nutt slowly raised his eyes from the compass and looked directly at Captain Phillips. "We're headed into bad waters, Capt'n. Bad waters."

John Phillips turned away and looked at the angry sea. "I don't believe in 'bad waters.' I don't believe in that mumbo-jumbo. It's all nonsense an' superstition talk, far as I'm concerned." He stepped to the rails and spit into the sea, then facing Nutt, shrugged. Next

Phillips looked to the mainsail and began to whistle loudly, and eyed Nutt. "The winds be whipped an' th' sea angry. Makes no difference what I do." He waved a hand over the cinders glowing at his feet. "Look at this. Did anyone do this? Nay. Just lightning. I've had my fill of lightning bolts, Mister Nutt!"

"But th' skies, Capt'n. Did ye see the skies at dawn? Red as a fireball. 'Sailors take warnin', as ye've heard," Nutt replied. "This," he pointed to the embers, "be bad luck."

"Hogwash!" Phillips turned his back on Nutt and, shaking a fist, shouted to the roiling sky, "I don't believe in bad luck an' I don't believe in you!"

"Bad waters, I say."

Phillips lowered his hand and pointed straight ahead. "Take us…there."

Twenty-Four

"I'LL WATCH OVER HER," EMANUAL Wynn said and moved deeper into the cabin. Seth followed. Charity recognized his tone—this was not a suggestion but rather a command.

She nodded and slipped outside, "As you wish."

Kathryn regarded the two pirates with distain. "I've trusted you both in the past but, for reasons I cannot say, I do not trust you now." She paused but got little reaction. "What are you going to do with me?"

Wynn regarded her for a moment and waited for Seth to take a seat on the other side. "That depends on you, missy."

"You will address me as Capt'n, Mister Wynn." Silence. Kathryn scowled. "And you, Seth...you stink."

Seth snickered at the insult, obviously directed to the belt he'd fashioned around his waist made from fish heads and tails. He did stink but didn't seem to mind it.

"Maybe." Seth laughed again.

"At least fish heads are less offensive than those eyeballs you nailed to the mast. You've gone mad, Seth. What's happened to you?"

Wynn cleared his throat. "This isn't about Seth, Kathryn. This little meeting is about you. We need to talk and ye've got some answerin' to do."

"Whatever you seek, you can find for yourself. I'm not sayin' anything…at least not to you! He's nutters and you're intrusive. Nothing I say will help my case, but likely incriminate me further." She shook her head. "And I've done nothing wrong!"

Seth's laugh sounded maniacal. "That's up for debate, Kat."

Kathryn knew there was little she could say that would sway the present company's opinion of her. Her sanity would remain in question until she could prove the entity was on board…and in the sky. *Everywhere! The evil surrounds us.* She shuddered at the thought.

"Are you ill?" Wynn sounded sincere. "You chill."

Kathryn shook her head. Wynn was fearless, had no sense of danger, only the sword. "No. As I said before," she eyed Seth, "I'm fine." Seth laughed out loud, spun in a circle with his arms extended, and hummed a tune she'd never heard before. "But he's not. Would you be so good as to get us both something to drink, Mister Wynn?"

Wynn's glance darted from Kathryn to Seth and back again. Nodding, he darted out of the cabin leaving Seth alone with her.

"Well, well, Seth. You've done it now."

Seth stopped moving and faced her. "You've no idea what's going on, Kathryn. My actions are for ye're own good. For the good of us all."

"But this was not the plan."

Seth spit at the floor. "The plan's the same, just altered a bit."

She walked a circle around him, studying him. Seth was clever, indeed—whenever he spoke of mysteries, usually there was a reason for it. Kathryn knew she couldn't take his comments lightly, but she realized he wouldn't spill information without prodding. "That's the trick then, eh?"

"What?"

"I know what you're up to, Seth," she bluffed.

His face blanched. "You know nothing, Kat, and that's in your best interest."

"You said that already." She circled him again. A dagger protruded beneath one leg of his trousers. She'd never seen Seth use a dagger but was certain he could. Perhaps his plan included taking her out.

Perhaps I'd best beat him to it. The thought soured in her mind but warmed her gut—a sure sign that intuition was at play. *Seth needs to die, but how to do it is the question. This must be handled delicately, or the crew will certainly revolt.* She eyed him and smiled.

"I suppose we have a lot to talk about then. Sit down, Seth. Sit."

He remained standing and watched as Kathryn retrieved a pistol from her skirting and held it in one hand.

Twenty-Five

I know what you're doin', Seth. It won't work. The thought hit him, and he glanced at Kathryn. She shook her head and moved closer. "Why the charade, Seth? No one buys it…at least I don't, and I doubt your beloved Capt'n Phillips does either."

"You don't get it, do you?" He faced her, glancing only briefly at the weapon in her hand. "If I can convince them I'm bat-crazy, the men give me a wide berth. I need to be left alone, Kat."

The comment caught her off guard and she stared at him, puzzled. "Why? What can you benefit from being so solitary? It seems you need the crew, need to be accepted."

He moved a few paces and screamed. "No!"

Kathryn startled and raised the pistol.

"No, Kat! I need space if I'm to pull off my plans."

She shook her head. "That's not part of our purpose. Have you forgotten the agenda? You'll ruin everything."

"To hell with the agenda. To hell with the purpose. To hell with all of this!"

She stepped closer. "Seth, remember why you were sent. Think of those in the future and how your impetuous selfishness will ruin it for them."

"You mean ruin it for you!"

She nodded and lowered her voice. "And for you as well…Brooks."

Silence fell between them for a moment. He swallowed hard and stared at her. In that moment, they communicated—in the silence—a knowing they shared from another century.

Suddenly, Seth lifted hands in a rather desperate move. "Your gonna kill me? Then do it," he shouted. "Get it over with for the both of us. Ruin yourself with the crew and, if you're not hanged, maybe Capt'n Phillips will make you governor of your own island to starve to death." Kathryn stood still as stone. "I've me own plans for the future, Kat. Like everyone else. Big plans…to get away…Capt'n me own ship."

"It'll never work, Seth. You don't have the experience. You're too…"

"Young? Is that what you were going to say? I'm too young?" The words tasted bitter. He spat again and wiped his mouth. "I'm the same age as you, *Capt'n Kathryn!*"

"You're forcing my hand Seth," she called after him, as he bounded up the steps topside.

She followed, still clutching the pistol. His sarcasm hadn't escaped her and stung as intended. A few of the men noticed the exchange and craned their necks to watch. Kathryn's look hardened as she stared down her friend. "I can't let you do this, Seth."

"Well, it seems you have no choice, Kat," he said, turning on his heel to face her. "No choice, my friend!" He nodded and smiled, then turned his back on her. The sarcasm was not lost on the men.

Kathryn watched him walk away and refused to wipe the tears from her eyes. She withdrew her pistol, took aim as the distance between them increased, and fired.

Twenty-Six

"Th' Capt'n's killt Seth!"

Several crewmen rushed to Seth's side, helpless, blood pooling, staining the deck where he lay. Cade nudged the body with his boot.

"Cold blooded murder," someone cried out as Wynn wrapped both arms around Kathryn, pulling her into him and knocking the pistol free.

"Leave it Kathryn," Wynn hissed. "Stop struggling!"

"Lass, what have you done!" John Phillips joined them, restraining her as well.

"Killed him, dead!" Wynn replied. "Seth…he's dead."

Kathryn relaxed and watched as Dobs picked up the smoking pistol. She tipped her head and he nodded, disappearing in the gathering crowd. She'd likely hang for this. It was inevitable. But the price was well worth it. They'd remember her as Captain and a true pirate. That was also inevitable…and necessary.

The shouting made its way to Bourn and Pedro. There was no mistaking the cries for help that scattered across the *Revenge*. Something horrid had happened and Bourn knew what that meant. The men eyed one another and darted aft to where the submersible remained hidden.

"Can't let anyone else see this, Pedro," Bourn said. His hushed tones did little to hide the urgency of the words. Pedro muttered something and nodded, taking up a position where he could see what the others were doing.

"Capt'n Phillips's there now. Dis bad, Bourn." Pedro's eyes grew wide. "Very bad."

"It'll be all right." Bourn reassured himself as much as the pirate blocking his view. "Wait it out, Pedro. That's all we do now…wait it out."

Men rushed past them, no one noticing Pedro and Bourn or the odd object they kept hidden. John Phillips' voice rose above the others, and Pedro ducked completely out of sight.

"What have ye done, Kathryn!"

She stood still as stone. The few men attending to Seth glanced from Phillips to Kathryn and back to Seth. Helplessness was soon replaced by hopelessness, palpable and terrifying. The healer had killed one of their own. Any one of them could be next.

Dobs kneeled beside Briggs, who held a wadded kerchief over Seth's bloody back. "Do something… please." Tears spilled over his cheeks as he bent over his friend.

"John Phillips is the carpenter aboard this vessel. He can do something." Kathryn shouted. Her voice sounded even more defiant.

Phillips raised his hand, and his eyes stared, lethal, fierce, ready to cut her down. "Witch!" He clenched his fist.

"Do it! Strike me down, John Phillips. But know this…it won't bring him back."

"Why Kathryn? Are ye so cold ye can stand by and watch him die?"

"If that is how it seems to you, then perhaps you are correct." She looked aft. "Fetch Bourn. He's the chirurgeon. He'll do what Mister Phillips will not." Behind her back, she tapped her thumb to her middle finger and offered a silent prayer. *It must work…it must!* She barely believed her own thoughts, but she was committed now and could not turn back. They were all committed.

Gow hollered for Bourn and ran to the back of the ship. Within minutes, he returned with Bourn at his heels. Saying nothing, Bourn scooped up Seth's body, glanced at Kathryn, then headed aft. Briggs and Wynn followed but Kathryn stopped them.

"Just you wait here. Bourn will handle this," she said. The men turned from her but stopped in their tracks. "I am still your capt'n. That's an order!" she barked. Kathryn then faced the rest of her crew. "That goes for all of you! Traitors die alone. Bourn handles the corpse, as he is not one of you…not yet. He has not taken the oath. I'll not have my crew soil their hands with a traitor's burial. Now, back to your duties!"

No one moved, all eyes on John Phillips. He glared at her then shouted to the men, "Ye heard her. Back to yer duties else face the yardarm an' cats. Handle th' crew, Mister Gow or give me the whip!"

Profanity rolled but the men obeyed. One by one, the crew returned to their tasks, each muttering something under his breath, mostly curses. And Kathryn knew she'd lost the loyalty of her crew. "Loyalty replaced by fear will do fine enough," she said to no one, then turned her back and headed aft herself.

Twenty-Seven

Pedro stood next to Bourn, murmuring under his breath in a strange language. Bourn assumed he was praying, likely Creole, but Kathryn knew better. As she watched from the shadows, she was certain he whispered the words of the Ogham.

"Help me, Pedro." Carefully placing Seth's body into the submersible, each man lifted an arm and gently placed an object beneath.

"This is for bounty and abundance in the next world, mate," Bourn said, and wrapped the loaf of bread he'd stolen into a rag, along with limes, figs, and salt pork, then placed it under Seth's arm.

"Dis be protection from evil." Pedro repeated the ritual, placing salt in a satchel beneath the other arm.

"Together we give sustenance for the journey, grog to keep ye lively and bless those spirits who greet ye at the gates o' heaven," Bourn said, glancing around them to see if anyone else could hear what they were saying.

Each man placed a jug in the bottom of the submersible near Seth's feet. Pedro closed the top and sealed it with pitch. Then, making the sign of the cross, Bourn nodded. Eyeing one another other, they hoisted the submersible to the rail and pushed it into the sea.

As the *Revenge* lurched forward, the submersible bobbed atop the rising crests. Within moments the currents had carried Seth's body far from the ship and her crew. Bourn crossed himself and Pedro bowed his head.

"Will it work?" Bourn whispered.

There was no response, except from the one who witnessed it all. She stepped out of the shadow and brushed her hands together.

"It is done. Now we wait," Kathryn said.

Twenty-Eight

THE SHOT SOUNDED FROM SOMEWHERE behind the gunwales. Only smoke rose, curling like horehound and honey in ribbons from the deck, the sparks from the blast immediately doused in the rainfall. As the ship pitched, another crack of light from the sky illuminated momentarily a figure standing in the shadows, pistol still raised and pointing directly at them.

Kathryn recognized him, the same silhouette from another occasion, another lifetime, when she'd fled the ghostly figure as he came for her on a beach.

"Archer!" she screamed. "How…who?"

Her legs crumpled and strong arms caught her as she collapsed.

"I warned ye, Mister Archer." The voice sounded distant, but she recognized it as belonging to John Phillips. Another shot sounded. Someone groaned and Kathryn heard the sound from within. "Confine him!" again from Phillips. "Bind the blaggard to th' mainmast. Gow stand guard!"

Kathryn lifted her hand to her belly and noticed its palm painted in blood. "I've been shot?" No one answered her question. Somewhere in the distance, men were shouting. It wasn't clear but perhaps another blast from a distant pistol, or perhaps lightning. She couldn't tell and allowed herself to sink deeper into the arms that held her.

"You're your own worst enemy Kat. You know that don't you?" Again, the familiar voice.

"Yes, I know," she whispered, as everything faded to black.

Twenty-Nine

BEES TEND TO SWARM WHEREVER they aim to settle, but just one of those tiny beasties with its lowly buzz makes even the most stalwart of souls freeze in place. This, too, was the crew's reaction, as if they sensed the danger humming around the *Revenge*, a hive of black energy that would not be stilled. The crew barely moved.

"So much darkness," Charity whispered. Her only response was a wide-eyed nod. "This is more than I bargained for, Danny," she continued. "Ye and Joseph owe more than ye promised. I did not agree to this… not this! I don't care who she is."

"Two shot in a single hour."

"Aye," Charity agreed. "Not what I negotiated."

Another nod. "You've got to tell her sooner or later."

A familiar rise of bile hit the back of Charity's throat. The update could destroy Kathryn, which would put their plans in a complete tailspin. It could never be. "Not yet. She's not ready to hear it."

Danny cast a knowing look, and Charity stayed silent. Together they sat and just listened for a moment.

"Why'd she do it?" Danny finally asked.

"Kill Seth or return? She didn't have to, you know."

Danny chewed on the thought, along with his bottom lip. His eyes darted from Kathryn to the bleak heavens. "Nothin' holy about that," he muttered under his breath. "This be dark magic, the like's I've not seen before. But a seer knows what it is, so they say."

"Tell me then, what is it? What's happening?" Charity's tone increased. "It'll all around us Danny. You're the seer. You said it yourself, 'A seer knows'… so, what is it?"

Another bolt of lightning cracked, and the *Revenge* pitched.

Pemberton shrugged.

"Her decision wasn't holy. Far from it, if ye ask me. She was savin' herself…maybe him," Charity tipped her hand toward Phillips. "The choice was hers an' she did it…ran straight into it without stoppin'."

Pemberton's sudden glance at Charity was more quizzical—it smacked of gossip-seeking, maybe even revenge. "Why do ye shudder so, Charity? Ye knew this might be the outcome. She has to know. Someone's got to tell her and ye've got the Capt'n's ear."

Charity spat. "Foul seas. Foul deeds. Fouled souls." She glanced from Pemberton to Danny. "This is more than she can bear. I haven't the heart to tell her but if I must… Curse ye both!" Charity wiped her mouth with her sleeve. "Yellow-livered vermin, both 'o ye! Too afraid to speak truth and so ye push it onto me. Ye're no better than the dogs Anne spoke of before she was captured."

"Curse us all ye'd like. Capt'n Kathryn deserves to know Anne's in jail, likely to hang…and I'm not going to be the one to get shot next tellin' her."

Pemberton agreed and took a step back. It was clear that of the three, Charity would have to be the bearer of bad news and tell Kathryn her cousin had been imprisoned in a Jamaican jail, along with the rest of Calico Jack's crew. All in wait for the gallows. Mary was there too. The whole of it soured Charity's mouth again as she thought of it.

"They'll hang Anne and Mary. That alone will destroy the Capt'n…likely kill her if blood poisoning doesn't."

"Likely fester and poison her blood," Pemberton said absently. "Save us the trouble."

Charity shot a look at the man who merely shrugged it off.

"He might be right on that account," Danny offered in defense. "One never knows."

"You're the seer, Danny. You're supposed to be privy to all of this!" she snapped. "But it doesn't take an oracle to see that if she dies, we all follow. Ye'd better pray she lives, that's all I'm sayin'. And it doesn't look good for her…or for us right now."

Thirty

KATHRYN HAD BEEN CONFINED TO her quarters with Wynn as guard. And besides, Kathryn had been shot. The ball had passed straight through the tendons of her hand and into her belly, leaving a nice hole in her flesh. Thankfully, all of her fingers moved as before.

"It's clean through her palm an' lodged inside her breadbasket. Yet still she lives! A complete miracle," someone had said upon seeing it. The wound had been bandaged as best as anyone could do, given the chirurgeon was nowhere to be found, and Bourn wasn't really a chirurgeon anyway. His disdain for the job was evident, so it was no surprise that he had gone missing.

In the meantime, the brig was rendered unusable, since the iron would no longer hold a prisoner. Archer had been tied to the mainmast, instead, with Dobs nearby assigned as guard, a grip on pistols should they be needed.

"The ship an' crew's gone to hell in a handbasket! An' if this storm doesn't take us out, the lunatics will." Dobs spoke to no one in particular, but anyone that heard him knew he spoke the truth. Archer laughed and Dobs raised one pistol to his face. "Nothin' out o' you, Archer. Yer as barmy as bats in the belfry, an' I'd be doin' everyone a favor to dispatch ye right here, right now!"

Archer grinned in response, his yellow teeth showing holes where several had been knocked out. The ropes around his body secure, he could do nothing but remain silent, the warning taken.

At the helm, Phillips noticed the interplay but left management of it to Dobs and, instead, turned his attention to the maps in front of him. "We'll offload on that island," Phillips gestured ahead to a tiny bump of land that disappeared with each crest of a wave.

"Aye, sir." Nutt turned the wheel, and the boat changed course—the islet now straight ahead. "Bearings 17 degrees North, 64 degrees West…"

"Thank you, Mister Nutt. Just get us there. What island is that?"

"From what I can tell, we're headed straight for St. Dominique. The isle is unknown to me."

Phillips nodded. "That will be just fine, Mister Nutt. We need land and quickly!"

"Aye sir."

"And we pray there's Obeah healers there."

Nothing more needed to be said. It was obvious to those who had sailed onboard the *Revenge* that a torturous shift had taken place, and not just the weather. Kathryn was shot and her mind fevered, ill from some sort of dark Caribbean magic…or at least it appeared so to some. To most, she was possessed. Either way, she endangered the ship. No wonder a woman on board was considered bad luck.

Upon taking her to the captain's quarters, and the solid door locked fast, a sprig of garlic had been hammered onto the doorcase and a line of salt spread along its footings. No one made claim to the task, and no one dared remove the charms. Even though she'd been shot and clearly incapacitated, the charms were unmistakably meant to keep Kathryn and her demons contained within.

The quarters, larger than most, closed in on Kathryn. She glanced around the room, noting the shadows deeper than usual, especially in the corners. Someone pulled off her boots and tossed them against the bed. As Kathryn had been relieved of all weapons, and the room apparently had suffered the same fate, she had nothing to claim except her books and the few chirurgeon's tools she had kept for herself. Of course, the hourglass sat in silence next to the picture frame Mariel had given her. "Fools!" she whispered to no one. "They don't know what they don't know."

Glancing up from where she lay, the picture frame sat in view. She looked to see only herself reflected in the portrait. *Where is everyone? Have they all abandoned me? Abandoned their Capt'n?* Perhaps the thought came from a fevered mind. She touched the bloody spot where a ball had entered. It burned.

Is this my blood?

Reaching above her, she pushed the frame alongside the hourglass. Still no one appeared and the frame spoke the truth she didn't want to acknowledge—revealing those who typically sustained and comforted her, loved ones, friends, Mariel, Winne, her beloved pirate captain, all fading from view. The numerous souls from earlier times had all dulled into blurry silhouettes within the portrait. Hers was the only clear depiction there.

They're pulling away from me. Apparently so, and I won't forget this betrayal, from the crew or from you! She turned away from the picture frame, her thoughts screaming as if the object were alive. The silhouettes floated behind her image there. "I…see…you," she whispered.

Out of the corner of her eye, the sight of something carved into one of the beams held her attention. Scratched in sharp strokes, the message was clear.

Forever yours, my K ~ J. P.

Forever, indeed. Until your bawdy redhead stows aboard. Kathryn spat. She glanced again at the portrait and saw the shadowed figure standing behind her fade a little more. Soon, she would stand completely alone—within the frame, within the confines of her life.

"So be it!" she hissed.

Thirty-One

The door swung wide on its axis, too rapidly for the hinges to make much of a protest. Their submissive creak served as a subtle reminder that someone had entered her quarters. Kathryn lay stock still. In hand, the intruders held rope and a single cat-o-nines.

"Is she dead?" one of the men queried.

"So, you've come to kidnap me once more, have ye?" Kathryn whispered. "I'm surprised you've the courage, Cade, after what happened to ol'e Flint."

Cade dropped his eyes to stare at the blood-soaked blouse she wore, then looked to the floor. "Aye, ma'am. These be me orders. An' I don't see th' cursed stone 'round yer neck, now, do I." He glared at her. "Consider this payback for me mate, Flint."

"Indeed." Kathryn coughed, and her wound oozed. "Well, then Mister Cade, do your worst. But remember there will be consequences whether I live or I die."

McMead stepped forward, brandishing a cutlass. Kathryn smiled. "Are ye so fearful of a dying witch that you flaunt your weapon, Mister McMead?"

McMead said nothing and lowered his blade. "Flint had it easy compared to what awaits you. Now, where's my guard? Where's Wynn?"

"He's been relieved o' his duties."

She coughed again and the blood stain grew larger. Just then, John Phillips stepped into the crowded chamber and pushed his way through the tiny mob. "Enough! Stand down."

Kathryn closed her eyes and laughed. "So, you've decided to do your own dirty work this time, Phillips? Wanted in on the fun, eh?" She heaved and caught her breath before continuing. "Kidnapping seems to suit you, methinks."

"This is no kidnapping, Kathryn, but if you'd prefer to call it that…"

"Oh-ho! How justifications do crop up when you're involved."

"The fever has reached your brain. You're not aware of what you say. I'm here to protect…" Phillips took a deep breath and waved off McMead. "We're taking you to someone who can help you."

It was obvious to Kathryn that they intended to take her by force, but there was little she could do about it. She'd decided long ago they wouldn't take her without a fight. She shook her head. "I don't think so."

Phillips gave the signal, and the men surrounded her. Kathryn's wrists were tied faster than she could reach for her dagger. John Phillips placed a hand on her back and lifted her onto a makeshift hammock, manned by Cade and McMead. They carried her up the causeway and onto the sun-soaked deck. The sunlight blinded her for just a moment. It would be her only break, and she hoped the pirates that held her were blinded as well. Whispering the ancient words of the Celtic warriors, she pled for strength to return to her body.

Then, she kicked, striking Cade in the knee. The crack that followed ensured he would not contend with her. He fell screaming. Almost instinctively, she turned on McMead, butting him in the head with her own. He stumbled, and as he did so, the tip of his blade caught Kathryn at the nape of her neck. Stifling a cry, she spun, ready to attack Phillips but falling back toward the deck instead. As she did so, she caught a glimpse of Cade writhing with his leg twisted and cock-eyed, his foot twitching nearly next to his shoulder.

John Phillips caught her just as she struck out again. "Stop it, Kathryn!" He wrestled her into his muscular chest and held her fast. Blood spilled from her wound, opening wider with each thrashing. Phillips side-stepped, nearly slipping in the gore. "Ropes. We'll need the ropes. She's wild as an untamed kelpie, she be, even injured!"

Nicholas Scala limped forward, quickly fastening a rope around Kathryn's arms. "What about 'er feet, Cap't'n?"

"He's *not your capt'n!*"

Scala ignored Kathryn and waited for Phillips' to answer. He did so with a nod, and Scala deftly tied her ankles as well.

"I'll carry her," Phillips said, hoisting Kathryn over one shoulder. She tried to fight against it, but to no avail. The pirates had taken her once again, against her will. Where to…she had no idea.

"I'll get you for this, John Phillips! You know me well enough to know I speak the truth!" The threat came from a voice weakened, ethereal. Kathryn spoke, yet it was not her voice. "You've seen a Celtic temper and what it can do. Release me. That's an order!"

Her tirade fell on deaf ears. As they loaded her into the dinghy, the rant continued, lessening in volume as the boat pulled farther and farther away from the *Revenge*. Men lined up along the rails to watch the dinghy withdraw, and said nothing. It was obvious the woman had lost her mind. It happened often at sea… many a good sailor went mad with nothing but the sea and superstition for company.

As the sun dropped to the horizon, the tiny island appeared darker than before.

"It's a sign…an omen," Bourn said, leaning against the rails, eyes on the dinghy that disappeared slowly, farther from the ship. "She'll be lost for sure."

"She's been shot! Of course, she'll die," Briggs said, joining them.

"Nay. De Jumbie got her. Obeah bush-doctor live da," Pedro replied, pointing to the island. "Dats de only way to fix dark magic."

And as he spoke, the sun disappeared blanketing the *Revenge* in darkness.

Thirty-Two

"Do NOT DO THIS, JOHN Phillips," Kathryn hissed from her seat in the longboat.

Phillips said nothing. Given the mood of their passenger, those at the oars followed suit, keeping silent rather than suffer the tongue lashing that she surely would deliver. Even the rudder mate remained quiet, as was the custom. She glared at each man, daring him to continue the expedition.

A second boat accompanied them—this one manned with a few of the crew, just in case the captive witch could not be controlled. It had not been Phillips decision for them to join, but he had not put up a rebuttal to their company either. Obviously, there would be more pirates who would make way to the island, but not until the coast was clear and Kathryn had been delivered to her conservator.

"Ye dare not look me in the eyes, then, Henry Payne, aye? The guilt you must feel at kidnapping an innocent woman must weigh heavy on your soul." Payne kept his eyes to the sea. "And you, Mister Bootman. You're no better. May you both—"

"Stop!" John Phillips turned on her, and the boat rocked wildly. "Ye'll not be castin' spells on me crew, Kathryn. Not this day."

"These men are *not you're crew*! They're mine and they'll do as I bid them or face the consequences." Though her threat sounded breathy and weak, the men recoiled.

Phillips leaned in close to Kathryn. "You're not this wicked, lass. Something's got hold of yer soul an' I mean to get it out." He took her face in his hands and readied for another round of cursing, even spittle from the woman. But, instead, he saw her eyes fill with tears. "Do ye remember the astrolabe I gave to ye?"

"Aye," she whispered.

"There's magic in it. It'll guide you to where ye're meant to be…guide ye to me." He paused and watched as tears stained her cheeks. She remained stock still, staring into his emerald-green eyes and feeling the warmth of his hands on her skin. It was a sensation she'd forgotten and longed for once. "Your resplendence is also your curse. You can't help it, I understand, but you must control it."

"I can't."

"That is why we're taking you to someone who can help."

The boat pitched and Kathryn moaned. Her injuries reminded everyone that she was human, and her body failing. Shouts were heard coming from the other jolly boat as Thaddius, Scala, and Combs shouted exclamations.

"Witch"

This was their rhetoric predominately, along with cursing and crossing themselves. Truly a dichotomy of superstition from the pirates.

"Necromancer!" Payne waved them off.

"No one can help." She bit each word as she spoke. "Abandoning me to an island won't solve anything either, neither will your ridiculous cursing."

Phillips sat back and studied her. It was obvious her wounds had fevered her mind so that she could not comprehend. Perhaps it would be wasted breath to explain. Perhaps not. "You'll not be abandoned, Kathryn. That, I promise you."

She let her head fall back and laughed, but the sound was more like the wail of a dying sea creature. "You have kidnapped me before and abandoned me, as well. I do not trust you."

There was no more to be said. She could not be reasoned with. As the island grew near, Kathryn muttered incoherent words of betrayal and Balor and love lost long ago. All of this was not missed by John Phillips. It was obvious she blamed him for her sufferings. The only hope for her lay in the darkness of the island. He prayed silently that the Obeah that lived there would help her.

What he didn't know was that the Obeah had a name.

Thirty-Three

THE CAVERN WALLS DRIPPED WITH something dark and red, glistening in the torchlight that Scala held just inside the entrance. Fog blanketed the ground, lapping at their feet but never leaving the lip of the cave.

"Evil in there, Capt'n. Pure evil." Scala said and withdrew a pace, leaving the cavern in darkness. "I'll not be venturin' in there." He rubbed a cross that hung from his neck.

Phillips stood still for a moment, glancing between Kathryn and the cave's opening. After a moment, he stepped inside, carrying Kathryn with him. Payne followed, torch in hand.

A low-pitched moan sounded deep from within and the men standing outside shuddered. Moments later, Payne emerged, drenched in sweat, trembling.

"It's in God's hands now."

Thirty-Four

"You can be right…or you can *choose* right." The Obeah circled her. "You know me, *Mellt Sosye.* I saw you from the Queen Anne's." She cast a look at Phillips. "An' you! You claim to be mates with others, even Edward. Yet I question your loyalty. Does it not bother you that so many abandon you?"

John Phillips said nothing. The Obeah walked to an alcove and lit something that cast heavy smoke and a bitter smell. "For you as well, be right…or choose right."

"Aren't they one and the same," Kathryn responded.

"Nay. One comes from the ego. The other from the soul." The Obeah lit a candle. Kathryn watched the light dance on the walls of the cave. "What beckons you, Kathryn the pirate?"

Phillips stepped between the Obeah and Kathryn. "When did you see me? What is your name, Obeah."

She chuckled, deep, throaty. "Some call me Babd, others Danu. You know me as Roane." Phillips felt a chill run down his spine. She turned to Kathryn and loomed over her. "I ask again, what beckons you, pirate?"

"Nothing. Nothing beckons me. I feel hollow." Kathryn replied.

Roane stared at the candle and watched Kathryn carefully through transcendent eyes. "You're hollow due to the fester." Then facing Phillips, "Leave us!" Hesitating for only a moment, he backed away, pausing at the opening in the shadows. "It's the only way to help her. She must face this alone, and you cannot be present. Now GO!"

He paused for a moment, but Kathryn nodded. In the next instant, John Phillips disappeared from the cave.

"Now, *Mellt Sosye*. Let's take a look inside you." Roane chanted, waiting for Kathryn's reaction. She fought back, holding tightly to the deep the truths she did not want to surface. Roane made the sound of a snake. "You cannot fight this and survive, pirate lady. You are consumed with hatred, by fear. It's eating you from the inside, like a parasite that nibbles and nibbles until nothing but putrefaction and decay remain.

"Yes!" Kathryn roared. "The fester, indeed. I cannot live with what he's done. The sight of them together…coupled…festers within my mind and I cannot let it go!"

Slowly, Roane turned from her. Kathryn's face flushed and her hands glowed.

"Where is the Seren?"

The question caught Kathryn by surprise. She hadn't noticed it was missing…not for a long time.

Grasping at her throat as if she could find it there, she shook her head and felt tears well in her eyes.

"Exactly as I suspected," Roane said and faced the candle again. "You've lost your strength, *Mellt Sosye*. You've turned from your calling." She touched the bloodied spot where the ball was trapped inside Kathryn's abdomen. "And it appears you've been shot, as well. Hmmm." She circled Kathryn and whispered ancient words. "Which hurts most…the damage to your body or the wound in your soul?"

Kathryn felt tears run the length of her cheeks. "I cannot answer. Both are painful."

"You must!" Roane snapped. "Or I cannot help you."

"But he lied to me! He and that red-headed tramp!" Kathryn spat.

The candlelight flickered violently against the walls, casting shadows that spiraled in a fierce angry dance of combat. Kathryn watched the gyrations, mesmerized as her anger seethed.

"Ah, then the soul is most injured." Roane raised a hand to stop her protest. "You bring the Capoeira," She gestured at the flickering light. "It foretells of war to come. A battle you fight at sea…and a battle you fight within yourself."

"But he lied— "

Roane spun on her heels; a godless stare leveled at Kathryn. "And you know this to be true?"

"I…"

"Are you a true witness of the accusation you make?"

The eyes of the Obeah burned her conscience, and Kathryn felt her skin ignite. Burning. *She's burning. She will certainly die.* The words seared into her brain from another time…another place. "I don't want to burn."

Roane said nothing, waiting for an answer that Kathryn did not want to give. "You have ignited the flame, *Mellt Sosye*. It dances there," Roane glanced at the shadows weaving inside the cave. The candle flame had come alive.

Kathryn could feel it crawling through her skin, igniting an old memory, and blistering her soul. "Make it stop."

Roane's maniacal laugh only added fuel to the fire. "This has nothing to do with me." She screeched again. "Answer the question."

Threads of smoke curled from Kathryn's skin. She could feel the embers just below its surface as blisters began to rise. Kathryn cried out. "I saw them together." Fire leapt from the wall, and she could smell her hair scorch. Burned into her memory, the image of Captain Phillips and Jacquotte Delahaye embraced on the bow of the *Revenge* would not leave her. She looked to the walls of the cavern and watched the same image played over and over again in dancing shadows. "I am the Capt'n now. I possess the *Revenge* and command her crew. I am—"

"You are not the *Mellt Sosye*, that is obvious. So, I will tell you another truth. You have chosen to burn alive in your self-created hell. Apparently, an easier fate than to face the truth."

Kathryn lifted her hands and stared at the smoke rising from her flesh. "This is more than I deserve, Obeah. Your words light a fire that encircles others like me. I don't understand what your purpose is…to ignite chaos and torture those who get in your way?"

"My purpose with you is only this," Roane responded. "To show you the truth, burn it into your soul if needs be and cleanse the hatred that's taken over there." She waved her hands above the smoke, carrying it with her to where Kathryn lay. "Your eyes are blinded by your anger and pride. That belongs to you. The *Revenge* does not." Kathryn opened her mouth to speak but Roane silenced her. "Look to the figurehead. Open your eyes and see. Therein lies symbolism you have missed for these many years." Roane threw her head back and laughed. "Of course, you missed it. You are no longer *Mellt Sosye*."

"I am…"

"You are nothing! That is another truth. As well, you must know that your beloved Anne Bonny is no more." Kathryn shrieked but could not move, her sinews charring beneath her skin. The musket ball's path glowing red-hot inside her belly. "Indeed, she is only missing—a far better fate than what befell Mary, her companion. Both were set to hang, along with that flamboyant, silly-mouthed Calico Jack they called a

Capt'n. It is said that your Anne called him a dog and fought nearly to the death before captured."

"Is she alive? Is Winne still alive?"

"Those who possess the twin ravens share the same fate. You were given one of the Ravens." Roane grabbed Kathrn's hands. "Where is it?"

"I gave it to the Vodoun priest as payment for…"

"Your power as *Mellt Sosye*. Yes. Yes, as I feared. And sadly, you cast it away to call yourself a Capt'n. Truly you are a pirate, Kathryn."

Kathryn curled her knees to her chest into the fetal position that waits for death. "I cannot bear this."

"Then face the truth. Winne is gone. Mary and Calico Jack dead, hung until their necks snapped." Roane laughed again.

"No!" Kathryn's voice was barely a whisper.

"And here is the last truth." Roane waved at the shadows. "You've lost everything and for nothing! You…the great *Mellt Sosye*…the one prophesied to defeat my sister, the Morrigan, is lost. All power lost. Gifts and protection, lost. The Seren, lost. Your pathetic Capt'n Phillips, lost. The *Revenge*, lost."

Kathryn looked at the cavern's walls and saw the shadows part. Her soul had known it all along, but her temper had blinded her. The shadows moved father and father apart. Her Captain and the wench, Delahaye had never been. Somehow, she knew they had never been. Everything she believed was a lie. A falsehood she'd told herself to appease her pride. Deep down, she knew the truth.

"You see it now. All for nothing. You are lost. You are nothing, Kathryn the Pirate!"

Thirty-Five

ALONG WITH THE FOG, THE stench of burnt flesh drifted outward, a fetid reminder of death and the dying. Behind it, the outcry of someone being tortured belched from the cave's opening. The pirates shrunk back, Henry Payne turned and lost the contents of his stomach into the nearest bush.

"Th' devil hisself be there, Capt'n," Dobs volunteered. "We best leave."

John Phillips stood stock still, peering into the black opening. A vision opened itself as fog encircled his boots. Images of pristine walls, sounds of something ringing or blasting…a beep, rhythmic, erratic. He heard the voice as clearly as if it was spoken aloud: *You're the one. You're the captain, aren't you?* He saw the shape of a woman take form in the fog, silver-haired and matronly. His own voice carried next: *Would you be the one to let her suffer so and prevent those who truly love her from going to her aid? Are you that heartless?* To one side, another stood, her face recognized by him in this time and another. "Wendy," he whispered, though he wasn't sure how the sound had come. Behind them, in the mist, the drone of a monitor tapped out a pulse. This was another place in a future time—one that he knew. *Hospital*, he whispered. Just then, the spectral shapes raised their arms as if beckoning something from within the cavern. Screaming sounded from far away. The older form turned slowly to look at him. She opened her mouth slowly. *Go!*

"This is why I came back. This is why I'm here." John Phillips' voice sounded flat.

"Capt'n?" Dobs could barely speak. "Don't… Capt'n."

"He's under a curse…hexed, he be," Scala said, "I knew this would happen!" Quickly turning on his heels, the Scala ran off. It didn't take another word for the others to follow, leaving John Phillips alone at the mouth of the cave.

Another wail roiled from deep within the cave. Death's rattle. The song of the dying. Someone whispered in Gaelic and Phillips felt it. The fog swirled, biting against the voices, tearing at Phillips' heels. In that instant, he knew his purpose. He had been sent from another time for this moment…for her.

The pirate faltered, blinking to regain his grasp on the present. Then, as if propelled by the whispered voices, John Phillips ran into the gaping cave's mouth and was swallowed by the darkness.

Thirty-Six

"Enough!" Phillips' voice boomed. "Release her, Obeah!"

Roane cackled and drifted opposite him, placing Kathryn between them. "She's done this to herself."

John glanced at Kathryn. Welts swelled her skin where smoke rose. *The stench of burnt flesh is hers!* It was clear that her life hung in the balance, but he wasn't sure what to do. Surely, he hadn't the power to change fate.

Or did he?

The pirate began to chant, mimicking the whispered voices he'd heard just moments ago. Gaelic words that only had meaning for Kathryn.

"Cluinn mi a-nis, a Chaitrìona...Lean mo ghuth.
(hear me now, Kathryn...follow my voice)

Tarraing air cumhachd an sosye leaghaidh
(draw on the power of the *Mellt Sosye*)

Agus gairmibh air na nithibh a tha
deanamh seirbhis dhuibh."
(and call upon the elements that serve you)

Roane cackled again and began to circle them. "Gaelic chants do not seem fitting of a pirate captain. I am surprised you have the courage to show yourself here, John Phillips, let alone speak the sacred words of the spellbinders."

Behind her, shadows leapt and twisted against the cavern walls, this time indiscernible as human or beast. Phillips kept his focus trained on Kathryn, unsure what to do next. The voices had stopped their whispering leaving him alone. *What now?* The thought remained unanswered.

Kathryn whimpered and he thought he heard her heartbeat. Again, the images of lights and beeping and people gathered around a woman lying on a steel slab. *My purpose…the reason I am here.* Roane cackled again breaking the trance, but he'd seen enough. He remembered why he had returned, and it was enough.

"Kathryn," was all that he said as he scooped her up, lifting her into his arms. And as he did so, a musket ball fell from her belly onto the floor. Then, John Phillips ran, with Kathryn in his arms, from the cave.

"Morrigan will know of this," Roane's voice echoed behind him. "She will hear of this, and she will know it was you."

Kathryn's skin blistered as he carried her. She was still on fire. "I don't know how to stop it," he said glancing down briefly. Tears welled and he feared what would happen if they fell. She was dying in his arms and there would be no mystical creatures or magic incantation to save her this time. "How do I help you, lass?"

As if in answer to his plea, the cave belched them into a cooler night air. Overhead, the stars formed a pattern that Phillips recognized. "The Straif," he said aloud. "Pedro will know." Holding her body next to his, he ran through the brush and prayed for something to stop the fire that burned within her. In that instant, the skies rumbled and soon shed its own tears.

With every drop that landed, her skin sizzled—steam rising from it in protest to the cooling drops that fell to abate the flame. She barely took in the sweet, cool air and he feared she may stop breathing altogether, but he remembered she lived and her heart grew stronger in that strange place with the lights and beeping sounds. *It was my voice! She heard it and…* He began to whisper in Gaelic once again.

Quickly, the ground became soggy, copiously saturated with water and the creatures that lived in it. He slowed his movement as he slogged through mud, watching for eyes or appendages that hunted humans. Cursing helped little, but he felt better for having said what he did—even in Gaelic the curse seemed fitting.

Then he stopped.

"Why didn't I see it before?" He glanced down at Kathryn. "It's you…the *Mellt Sosye*! The four powers of the *Mellt Sosye*."

Looking back to the sky, John Phillips held her outward as if to receive the rainfall.

"Water."

Then reaching down into the mud, he scooped a handful and smeared it across her arms and face.

"Earth."

As if the elements understood they had been called, a gust of wind blew across them both, leaving him in no doubt that the powers of the Celts had been summoned.

"Air."

Lastly, he whispered a final dictum. Gaelic phrases carried on the wind and called the last element to her.

"You, lass, be the Fire."

A crack of lightning seared the sky, striking trees and sending a glowing blue of current along the boggy ground. The current hit them both, surging within the capillaries of his arms and through to his hands. He glanced down, realizing there was no pain, but the markings that showed along his arms took the pattern of ferns and feathers. He was, indeed, marked.

Thirty-Seven

"Lightnin'-buggars. That's what they be." Slade nodded at the markings on John Phillips back and arms.

"Aren't called that. I knows for certain. Met th' man it's named after," Dunkin stated.

"I seen 'em before. They're called 'Lightnin'-buggars'."

"Not what they're called. I met the man in person, I did."

Slade shook his head. "Ye're dreamin', mate. Ye've never met no man what knows these marks… looks like a ruby tattoo, to me." He pointed to John Phillips forearms where the ruddy, feathered marks stood out abruptly against his tanned skin. "Light—nin'-bug—gars!"

Phillips had grown irritable with the bickering. "What in Hades-Halls are they, then, Mister Dunkin?" He turned to look over his shoulder at the feathery pattern that ran along his arm and onto his back.

"Lichtenberg figures…at least that's what Mister Lichtenberg called them."

Slade snorted. "Of course he did. Named it after himself."

"He's a science man. Prussian. Studies these things, he does. I know…I met him off the Bay O' Biscay. He'd been in France and…"

"Didn't. Liar says I." Slade spat. "Why'd a tar such as yerself meet a science man, anyway? No reason! No reason anywise!"

"Did so. Has a twisted back, big hump right 'ere…" Dunkin pointed.

Phillips jumped to his feet. "Enough! Take yer bickerin' elsewhere. An' if it come to blades, I take the first strike."

"Aye!" sounded feebly from both men as they scooted off.

"Mind yerselves!" Phillips shouted after them.

While they did not cause pain, the marks on his back and arms blazed a bright red, fern-like pattern. Phillips had heard of this before but had never really seen it—assuming, instead, that the tale of lightning strikes leaving a mark such as these was merely superstition. Apparently, he was wrong.

"Bloody feathers!" Phillips cursed and replaced his shirt to cover the pattern that stood out through the fabric. A soft moan sounded from the bed, and he turned his attention to where Kathryn lay. Her skin bore the same marks, trailing across her chest and up to her throat. The smell of burnt flesh still hovered about her, though her skin showed slight improvement. She was healing, or so he hoped.

"Capt'n?" The voice came from the other side of the doorway and Phillips wondered if it was meant for him or the woman lying on the bed. "Capt'n? Might I come in?"

"Aye." Phillips responded and glanced up to see Pedro step over the threshold.

"She bad." It needn't be said but seemed appropriate. "She unda da curse."

"Aye, she's bad. I don't know how to help her, Pedro. She'll die if…" Phillips swallowed back the thought and stood to look out the glass quadrangles that served as windows. The island, still visible a short measure from where they'd anchored off, glistened as sand caught moonlight in its tiny elements. From where he stood, the island looked less menacing than Phillips knew it to be. Shadow magic lay hidden in the depths of that island…dark voodoo—the kind that, once tried, most can never return. "Where is the crew?"

Pedro stood silent for a moment, glancing occasionally at Kathryn, fear behind his eyes. "She bad," he repeated.

"I know that, Pedro. I just don't know what to do about it!"

"Cap't'n, a few o' dem disappear, don' wan' to be aboard the ship wit…" He glanced again at Kathryn. "It be dangerous, dey say. Obeah cursed her…an' curse da ship along with 'er."

"Lily-livered, black-souled pups!" Phillips kicked an empty pail, exasperated. Its clatter only added to the tension in the room. "They fear the stories more than what they see with their own eyes. Superstition! That's all this is." He waved a hand at Kathryn and caught sight of Pedro's stare. "She's sick, Pedro! That's all. And she's been shot with no one to care for her, except us. She's the chirurgeon for th' crew but has none for herself. So, of course she's worse than…than…" His voice trailed off, unconvinced of his own story.

"A few stay. Most plan to board a different boat, sail under new colors, dey say."

"I see." Phillips kept his gaze focused on the island in the distance. They could pull anchor soon, under the circumstances. "Who be it that abandons th' *Revenge?*"

Pedro dropped his gaze to the floor. "Too many, sir. Trouble's ahead an' the crew's stayin' ashore. I…I be joinin' them too."

"Pedro! Friend! You take leave of me, of yer ship, of yer crew?"

Pedro turned his back to John Phillips and walked to the doorway. "Dis not be yer crew, an' yo not be da cap't'n."

"Rude of you. Pedro! I took ye in. Took ye under me care an' gave you equal shares."

"Aye." Pedro kept his gazed trained to the floor.

"Then how can ye do this. How can ye abandon me…abandon the *Revenge* like this…now, at the time yer needed most."

"She requires magic to cure dis curse. Magic stronger dan de Obeah." Pedro shook his head. "I don' know where yo find it, but it's not here, not on dis ship." He lifted the thick black rod and held it out to Phillips. "Maybe dis. Maybe da Straif help her."

Phillips took hold of it and ran his fingers along the etched symbols. "This belongs to her. I don't know how to use it." Pedro remained silent. "I'm asking you as your capt'n to stay."

"Yo not da cap't'n." Pedro stepped to the causeway and pulled the door closed behind.

Thirty-Eight

"TAN KAP VINI AN POTE dlo nwa ak syèl nwa." The Vodoun priest's eyes grew wide as smoke encircled his head. His stature was small, withered in fact, but his power commanded the forces of nature without question. Phillips felt admiration and fear at the same time as he watched the little priest wave his arms and sprinkle powder into the tiny flame. Blue and green sparked for a moment before settling back to a bright yellow flicker that sputtered, and eventually died.

"What'd he say?" Phillips asked.

Scala shuffled his feet. "Well, I think he said something to the effect that her future is bright, and the sky is blue, fair winds, time to get to sea…something like that."

Phillips stared at Scala.

"That's not what he said."

John Phillips looked around for the speaker. "Who said that?"

Danny whispered, "I did, sir," averting Phillips' stare. John Phillips closed the gap between himself and

Danny. The man trained his eyes to the deck, refusing to look directly at Phillips. "Scala got it wrong."

"Then what did th' man say? An' be cautious ye speak th' truth."

Danny took a deep breath and looked up into John Phillip's eyes. "He said, 'The future brings dark water and black skies.' I swear on me life, Capt'n Phillips. It's known as *Kakés Moirai.*"

Silence felt heavy between them. Phillips could only stare at Danny, unable to comprehend what just had been said. A few of the others began the black-spot ritual, spitting and hopping on one foot. They all knew it wouldn't help…not this time.

Finally, Phillips spoke. "I know *Kakès Moirai.* This does not bode well…not for any o' us." He glanced aft, to the place where Kathryn lay below deck. "If she dies…we all die. It will be a bloodbath, mates, the likes we've never seen before. Not even when the creature took the heads of our crew three years past."

As if calculating the souls of each man standing before him, the old man raised his yellowed eyes and glared at Phillips. He lifted a gnarled finger and began to draw in the ash. A single loop that wove over itself in a pattern of three emerged. "*Triskele a.*" The withered priest pointed to the symbol in the dirt. "*Here…Li pote repons lan.*" He tapped the image and waved at Phillips to move closer.

"What's he sayin' now?" Phillips said, hesitating as he bent down to look at the image. Not wanting to get closer, Phillips gave him a warning look but the yellow eyes only stared in earnest and the man nodded.

"I…I think it's a symbol or somethin' akin to… It doesn't make sense, Capt'n. He says it be 'th' answer'." Danny shook his head.

The priest tapped at the symbol again and leaned in as if to whisper. "*Straif la pote soulajman ak lapè sèlman nan Mellt Sosye la.*" He grinned with teeth blackened from years of chewing the betel nut. Phillips smelled the clove on the old man's breath. "Here. Look closer."

The old man planted the palm of his hand flat against John Phillip's crown, nearly pushing Phillip's nose into the ash, stopping only inches from the mark he'd made with his finger. There he saw it.

Phillips gasped and sat upright. "The triskele."

The priest dropped his eyes to the triskele drawn in the ash and motioned for Phillips to pay attention. Reaching a gnarled finger downward, he drew a fourth swirl next to the others, then glanced up at Phillips, waiting for comprehension to set in.

The other men leaned in a bit, as if inches would help them see better what they'd already viewed. Phillips waved them away and glared at Danny. "Tell me exactly what the old man said just now. And don't leave out a single word."

Danny swallowed. "It brings th' answer. I think he means that…" Danny motioned to the symbol in the dirt. "Th' trisk…whatever ye said, Capt'n."

"Triskele."

"Aye. Triskele brings th' answer. The Straif…" Danny shrugged. "…brings relief an' peace, but only to the *Mellt Sosye*." He shrugged again.

John Phillips' face blanched. He bowed to the priest, tossing a few coins onto the symbol in the ash, and stood. The voodoun priest snatched up the coins, oblivious to the pirates that stared wide-eyed. "Get him back to shore, and someone clean up this…this mess." Phillips said waving a hand at the bones and ash that had been heaped there.

"Aye" came the response, as Pemberton took the priest topside, followed by Danny. The others waited for orders, afraid to touch the relics left behind in ash. No one dared move. No one knew what to do. It would take a someone brave enough to command the sea and the ship to snap the men out of their stupor—someone who didn't believe in superstition and a seafarer's folklore.

Phillips grunted, snatched his hat, and turned on his heel. "Come men. We have work to do."

Thirty-Nine

SUDDENLY, EVERYTHING MADE SENSE.

Phillips bounded up the short causeway leading from the quarterdeck to a cluster of men pouring over the navigation maps. "Fetch Archer." The urgency in Phillip's voice left Gow frozen, stock-still. "Now, Bosun!"

"Aye," came Gow's response.

Several pairs of eyes studied Phillips. "Quit yer starin', men. Ye've work to do if we're to set to sea."

"But the Capt'n..?"

"You're lookin' at yer capt'n, an' with disrespect, it appears." The comment did not go unnoticed. "Drop the bilge-talk and listen to me. We've work to do if this ship is to be ready. Now get to yer duties!"

John Phillips scanned the ship, hoping for some sign of Pedro but there was none to be seen. He was a man of his word and was gone. *Sad parting from a good mate, methinks.* The thought left him feeling unsettled. Perhaps more crewmen would follow suit. There was little he could do about it, at this point. "Best leave off it," he said aloud.

"Leave off what?"

Phillips was surprised to see Charity Vane standing so nearby. "What did you hear?"

"Only that ye think it best to 'leave off' someone or something."

He sighed. "Well, if you must know, I've lost one of me best crewmen. Apparently, Pedro's spooked by…by…"

"By what?"

"By…" he waved his hand in no particular direction but glanced up at the still angry skies. "…by all o' this."

"Ahhhh," Charity nodded. "He's not the only one, Capt'n Phillips. There are many in the crew who think the ship is hexed, some say jinxed. Either way, it's bad luck to be aboard the *Revenge*, they say."

"Who say? What yellow-bellied bilge rat believes such superstitions about me ship!"

Charity studied John Phillips for a bit, then put some distance between them. His Welsh temper had flared and she wanted no part of it. "Well, Capt'n Phillips—and let me just say that I would've enjoyed sailin' under yer colors, I would. There be several men, and women…" Charity ducked from the glare Phillips shot at her. "…aye, myself included, that think we'd do best on our own…elsewhere, as it were."

"Oh, ye do, then, do ye?"

"Aye. It's not personal to you. Most every man… and woman…aboard think you're one o' the best capt'n's to sail the Caribbean Seas, but the ship."

"What about the ship? Speak plainly, Lass!"

"It's cursed…because of her. None o' us wish to risk another voyage under these skies and that water. It's angry, fiercely so! There's too much risk in it." Charity dropped her gaze to the deck.

"I see. And how soon will ye and the crew abandon yer ship?"

Charity let that barb go. "Immediately. We've already gone ashore, most of us. I just came back for this." She held up a tattered knapsack that held worthless belongings, most likely priceless to Miss Vane.

"Who else joins you in this?"

Charity dropped the knapsack. "Well, there Featherston, Davis, and Howell already joined Jack Rackham's crew. They left a while ago. Nobody missed 'em after they left, though."

"What? For Calico Jack's crew!"

Charity smiled. "But I've heard rumors. There's nothin' good about Rackham's fate. The William was broadsided, damaged badly, an' the crew captured, including the colorful Calico Jack…" Charity smiled. "…was taken prisoner in Jamaica. No one escaped, from what I've heard."

John Phillips shook his head. "Foolish of Rackham. Foolish indeed. Likely, he put up a fuss."

Charity stared, unblinking, unsure whether to continue the account of Calico Jack's demise or go on with the list of abandoning crewmen. She decided on the latter. "Then Earl, Dobbins and Harwood, and Bourn—"

"Bourn is leaving? He's abandoning Kathryn?" Phillips started to pace. "This is incredulous! She'll never forgive him."

"He's going out on his own with Pedro, as you know. Cuddy too!"

"Well, fare thee well to all o' them. May the seas be friendly and the skies fair, although methinks they'll likely find foul weather and folly…or the hangman's noose awaits," he sneered.

Charity cleared her throat. "And there's one more thing ye ought to know, Capt'n Phillips. It's about Anne Bonny."

Forty

"She's dead. Likely from childbirth, so they say, in prison."

"Mary Read is dead?"

Charity nodded. "Aye. Saved her from the noose, though, or so rumor has it. It's been the talk o' the town." Phillips gave her a look. "Aye, well, the island then…not really much of a town, truth be told. But word travels fast an' these natives be willin' to share a juicy piece o' gossip for a piece…" He glanced at her again, wide-eyed this time. "…a piece 'o eight!"

"They were captured?" John Phillips eyes narrowed. He could hardly believe what he heard. "All of them?"

"Aye, Capt'n." Charity feigned a tear. "Th' *William* laid anchor off Jamaica Isle an' was spotted by a someone called, Barnet who called for th' *William* to strike her colors. Of course, Calico Jack refused, and Barnet hit them with a broadside. Rackham ne'er put up a fight upon capture…too drunk or sommat like that. Just the women braved the sword an' fought like mad dogs."

John Phillips began to pace. "This is bad news, bad news indeed. Were they kilt outright?"

"Oh, nay, sir. It's said they all been captured, escorted to prison, where Mary died in childbirth, or so they say."

Phillips stopped his pacing and stared, stock still, at Charity. "And of Anne Bonny?"

"She disappeared. Claimed to be with child, as well…to likewise spare her from the noose. But she disappeared altogether before the birth and the hangman never got to her."

"Where is she?"

"No one knows for certain. Just up and disappeared into thin air, they say." Charity smiled.

Phillips breathed a sigh of relief. "Calico Jack Rackham could always be counted on to be the cowardly, yellow dog that he was."

"Jack Rackham is dead, sir."

Phillips said nothing.

"I said, he's dead. D-E-A-D…"

"I heard ye, Charity Vane. And I'm fully aware of whence yer name comes from. Ye must have a kinship to Capt'n Charles Vane who commanded the reckless Calico Jack. No wonder he's yellow-bellied, foul…"

"No sir…I mean, yes, Capt'n Vane is relation. But I've no fondness for either Capt'n Vane or Calico Jack. Not at all! Methinks the noose fit him proper, it did. Hung in Jamaica for all to see. He an' a few of his men. I hear th' birds pick at his bones in the gibbet at Gallows Point in Port Royal."

"Were the defectors part o' the captured?"

Charity shook her head. "I cannot say, but I did hear that Howell, Earl, Dobbins, and Harwood met their end the next day. Fenwick too."

"Shame," Phillips shook his head again. "Those men had a fine arrangement here under my command. If they had just held onto their agreement, th' oath they swore."

Charity began to gather up some of her belongings, including her cutlass. "Aye, true. But on the wrong side o' the noose, they be, and ye're not Capt'n officially, an' the men sense the same. Meself, well, I feel uneasy about our prospects aboard the *Revenge* now." She paused only to stuff her cutlass in her belt. "Each man's got to look after himself now. Especially with th' Gov'nor's decrees and British navy takin' over the waters these days."

There was little Phillips could say. The news would destroy Kathryn. "What of Bourn?"

Charity shrugged and walked away. "No one's heard of him, or Pemberton or Danny or…"

"They never came back? Those two bleggards took the priest to shore on my command and never returned?"

Charity nodded. "Apparently so. They said that…"

"Enough! I get yer meanin'. Go, and good riddance to ye all."

Phillips watched as Charity walked down the gangplank, trailed by a few others. His eyes followed his crew as they abandoned his ship, something as captain he would never forget…or forgive.

Forty-One

"HEAVE!"

As soon as Briggs shouted the order, the waves slapped back, and the *Revenge* rolled. It would be a hard night. With few men to man the ship, the work would be difficult and long. Of course, those who remained loyal to the ship and John Phillips manned the lines.

"Heave!" The call repeated and the men responded, "Ho!"

Nutt approached Phillips, although rather timidly. He obviously wasn't sure where his loyalties lie and none who stayed on board wanted their necks in a noose…at least not yet.

"I don' think we'll manage wit' just these 'ere, Capt'n." Nutt's face scrunched sourly against the rain. "Not possible, sir."

Phillips' lips curled into the familiar half-grin at the title his navigator gave him. It was true, the men still looked upon John Phillips as their captain, even if they were afraid to say so to any of the others. Phillips clapped Nutt on the back. "Let me worry about that,

Mister Nutt. Ye'd best stay focused on yer maps. Keep us free from any British crosshairs, aye?" He winked and Nutt's face soured again. It was obvious that while the men still looked to Captain Phillips to lead them, they didn't trust him entirely, not just yet.

"Aye," Nutt replied. "But what of…?" he nodded behind them.

Phillips' gaze followed. "She's quiet now. Cook gave her sommat to keep her calm." He looked up, blinking his eyes against the storm and the flash of another lightning bolt. "Can't say the same for th' squall. That we'll have to ride out, Nutt. It's up to you to keep the ship upright an' on course."

"Aye, aye, Capt'n."

Captain Phillips grinned again and called out orders. Men jumped to their duties and the ship seemed to be back to its normal functioning as they prepared to make sail. Still, faces lifted to glance at the black haze overhead and several flinched at the thunderous crack of each bolt from deep within the folds of rolling cloud cover. These were not sent from a typical Caribbean squall—these were intimidations, threats, even warnings from the sky gods to any sailor who dared cross this part of the Seven Seas. Something ethereal was angry and it seemed to be focused on the *Revenge*. Even so, Captain Phillips pressed the men to get underway. Landlocked vessels only met with complete annihilation when tempests such as this one threatened.

"Archer, Capt'n," Gow stated, joggling Phillips from his thoughts. He shoved the wild-eyed prisoner forward, hands bound behind his back. "Caught him forward, foragin' through th' armament supplies. He's no business bein' in there! No business, says I."

Phillips eyed Archer. "Ye tied him up, then, did ye, Mister Gow?"

"Aye, that I did."

"Weapons?"

Gow shifted his weight and puffed out his chest. "Relieved of them firstly."

"Fine work, man!" Phillips' eyes never left Archer's as he slapped Gow on the back, "Fine work indeed, Bosun," then began to circle Archer as if inspecting livestock.

Archer spat. "Get on wit' it then! What's me fate? Noose? Cats?" He spat again, this time hitting Phillips' boot. "Run me through then, an' get on wit' it, says I!"

Phillips wiped his boot on the back of Archer's calf. "Impressive aim." Then, circling again, he stopped. "Ye were once a superior Quartermaster, and I once be proud to call ye mate. But sommat's happened to ye, John Rose Archer, and I cannot have ye onboard me ship."

Archer said nothing.

"You've leave to go, an' the men won't lay a hand on ye per my word. This out of respect for your past position on the *Revenge*. Still, ye owe me…owe yer mates," Phillips continued.

"What, then? What do ye want, John Phillips?"

Phillips took a deep breath then softly asked the question that had been hounding him for the past three years. "Why Kathryn?"

Archer began to howl, a lunatic's laughter. "That is what ye want from me? Yer all simple-minded fools."

Phillips stared hard, waiting, and Archer's eyes grew black.

"That witch comes from another world. She's a necromancer…a banshee. Th' fourth of three." Archer screeched again. "Ye still don't understand. Kathryn is the fourth sister…th' one that completes th' Morrigan. If…when she joins the others, th' Morrigan's whole again, an' there's no stoppin' 'em. They'll all be after ye, th' imposing Capt'n John Phillips!"

John Phillips stood as stone; his emerald eyes flaming as he stared down his former quartermaster. "Get this vermin off my ship!"

Gow snatched one arm as Slade grabbed the other, dragging Archer midships. Cries to "Throw 'im overboard" followed them, tempting—a fitting end for one such as the madman Archer.

"I've seen her. In the fog, I saw her there. Another time, another place. Followed her, I did. Watched her move in a vessel that sailed over black roads." Archer cried out again. "Left me handprint on her glass window, I did. She knows me. Another time…another place, it be."

Archer was flung from the *Revenge*, landing hard in a dinghy. Any other man would have suffered from the fall but not Archer. Alone, he rowed the short distance to shore with strength unbefitting his worthless body. And when he stepped foot on the sand, the crew watched as a wild animal emerged from within his soul, and the infamous John Rose Archer scampered off on all fours into the brush, never to be seen again.

Forty-Two

THE MEN STOOD READY FOR orders, and though they were few, they were mighty. A new strength advanced over the *Revenge* as it repelled John Rose Archer. The plague that followed him was gone, absent from the ship and the crew. Captain Phillips noted the shift and readied himself for what he would next do.

"It's time I take back me position as yer Capt'n an' we once again dominate the Caribbean Seas." He paused, hands on hips. "What say ye, my fine crew?"

"AYE!"

"Well, then, men. We've naught but few to man this fine vessel an' ye know we'll need more hands. What say ye we find us a fine sloop and invite her crew to join us?"

The sarcasm was not lost on the men, who whooped and danced at the thought of a long-awaited plunder. These days, the Caribbean was full of ships, all for the taking by skilled pirates, and Captain Phillips' men were skilled, indeed.

Just then, a large bolt of lightning cracked, nearly hitting the mainmast. Rain soaked and with renewed hearts, the flash lit up their weathered faces.

"To yer posts. Let's advance this lady, farther, deeper to sea where she belongs!" Captain Phillips roared.

"Ho!"

As if she knew, the *Revenge* lurched, taking her crew into deeper waters. The journey had just begun, and it seemed as if the ship wanted to obey Captain Phillips' orders as well. Overhead, the blackened skies emptied itself in torrents that stung as the deluge hit bare skin. But the pirates had other things on their minds, mostly thoughts of plunder and marauding misdeeds. Truly, their spirits had lifted, in spite of the dismal climate, and the sea beckoned in response.

As night flourished and the wee hours of the new day crept forward, the crow's nest quaked, alerting Dunkin, who gave the signal. "Ship, ahoy, portside bow!" Instantly, the crew took to their stations, ready for battle. There was no need for an order this time.

Standing ready at the capstan, Gow kept his eye on the captain, ready to relay any order that would follow, but none did. The men were prepared for whatever Dunkin had seen, and everyone knew it. Their confidence was soon rewarded when a flash from lightning lit up sails in the distance.

"Galleon! Portside!" Dunkin called out again. "Spanish."

"The Fleet?" Slade whispered but no one answered.

Should this be a Spanish galleon, the pirates would be fortunate, indeed. But taking a ship from the Fleet of the Indies would be formidable.

"Across the bow! Let 'em know we're here and ready!" That first shot was a warning. The next would spell out the pirates' intent. "Make it count, men. Take 'er midships an' then aim for the mast."

Shot after cannon shot flew from the *Revenge*, as if propelled by the devil's own hands. At least six rounds hit their target before the Galleon retaliated. Within minutes, the skies were alight with cannon fire, and despite the unforgiving downpour, fires ignited on both ships as a result.

"Deal with that, Mister Scribbs, an' make haste else we all burn wit' the ship!" Gow shouted the order and several men stepped up to douse the flames with their buckets.

Another volley from the Galleon threatened to ignite the *Revenge* midships, landing too close to the capstan. Lightning cracked, matching the deafening snap of fractured wood. The *Revenge* suffered an onslaught from the Galleon, but she held fast, and the crew worked feverously, in spite of their small numbers. Still, there were too few men to handle the constant volleys from the larger vessel.

Another blast shattered the mizzen mast and sparked flames to its sails. "Fire!" the cry sounded from somewhere aft, but the water buckets did little to impede the ever-growing flames. "She'll burn! Fire to the mizzen sheets!" Smoke-addled voices cried out in desperation.

Suddenly, the air compressed, and a low rumble sucked all sound from the *Revenge*. A blue current radiated outward, crossed the deck and passed over the sea water.

She had emerged.

"Ale antite. Mwen mande pwotèktè yo pou yo veye bato sa a ak mesye sa yo." As her voice was but a whisper, and as she commanded the entities to depart, she called upon the ancient Celtic protectors as sentinels for the ship. "Netwaye dlo sa yo epi mete separasyon ant nou ak lènmi nou yo."

No one dared speak. And as they watched surges of electricity move from her outstretched hands to cross the sea, the men dropped their weapons one by one and the flames died out. Captain Phillips stared at her, and a smile crossed his lips.

"Indeed," he whispered. Moving slowly to return his gaze, she raised her hands, as if to remind him who was in power. He nodded. "Kathryn comes back."

No one needed to be told. No one needed reminding. The *Mellt Sosye* had returned.

Forty-Three

Damage to the galleon was significant. Likely, with the repairs needed, the larger ship would have to be scuttled.

"It's tragic, pure an' simple," Slade said, then spit on the deck. Luck was scarce these days, and he didn't want to cross out his remaining windfall.

"Aye." Gow crossed himself, warding off any evil spirits that might lie between him and the spoiled prize. "She'd have made a good addition to our fleet."

Slade shot a look at Gow. "Fleet?"

"Well, it might be a good plan. Capt'n should build up our presence, so-to-speak."

"We don't have enough men to work th' *Revenge* as it is! How can we operate a fleet?" Gow said and glanced at the burning galleon. "She's done-for anyway. That's all I'm sayin'."

The longboat pitched and Slade dug into the current harder. His oar seemed to do little against it. Overhead, the sky cracked again, and lightning tickled the sea. Several of the crew manning the boat ducked, as if that would save them.

"She's angry," Slade said. "As if she knows we're here."

"Of course she knows! She's gatherin' up the souls of the dead…there…on the burnin' ship," Scala replied.

"Morrigan!"

"Aye…an' we're goin' right to her!" Scala nodded at the galleon. "Why not just let her go…let her sink to the depths of the sea an' leave it well enough alone?"

"Because there's booty an' plenty of it in her holds." Gow smacked the water with his ore to make a point. "We'll take what's ours an' leave the ship and souls to… to…*her*."

With a few additional strokes, the longboat reached the incapacitated galleon. Ash and cinder fell aft from where her stores had blown. Fortunately, the Spanish Treasure Fleet rarely stowed their most precious cargo near the gunpowder for just such incidents as this. Should the ship falter and the powder be blown, at least the crew would have time to salvage the silver that was held near the forward bow, next to the precious previsions used for survival.

As the pirates cast their hooks into the sinking ship's rails, few of the Spanish soldiers took notice, and those who did cared little for the pirates' plan to board. Captain Phillips' longboat joined Gow and his men, calling out orders to "Prepare to board!"

Smoke from the fires stung their eyes and the pirates sensed they'd have to hurry to get the provisions and plunder held there. Bracing for conflict, the pirates raised their weapons but soon realized there would be no fight. Every man on board dashed for the same trophy: doubloons and silver coin.

No one stopped the pirates from plundering. No one interfered with the Spaniard's attempts to save their souls. *Every man for himself* seemed the theme of the moment, and overhead, the skies dropped buckets of oily-black rainwater slickening the decks so that men often lost footing and slipped through broken rails, lost at sea. And all the while, the Morrigan fed her hunger for men's souls.

But it was never enough.

As Kathryn watched from the *Revenge*, she felt the fading heartbeats of those dying men, now gripped in the clutches of her adversary. In silence, she watched as the spirits rose from the water toward the darkened skies, only to be snatched into the gaping mouth of the soul-eater. Morrigan's ghastly image contorted and twisted, her once beautiful face becoming beastly as she gnashed and snarled at dead men's souls.

As she looked upon the grisly spectacle, Kathryn felt no anger. Nothing. Her soul was unrestricted and her mind clear. Finally, from the fiery purge that overtook her in the cavern, she was free.

"Take what you will, Morrigan, but my men and my Capt'n Phillips, ye shall not." Kathryn lifted her hands again as she spoke. A blue firebolt shot from her hands and quaked the waters.

Forty-Four

"Avast, men!" the cry came as several of the *Revenge's* crew were thrown into the air and into the water. One by one, each found a longboat, bobbing alongside the Spanish galleon. Still intact, the men scrambled inside and clenched the oars.

"Pull! Pull with all ye've got, men! As if our very lives depend o' it!" Gow's voice shook as he called out orders.

Captain Phillips was last to climb aboard the second boat, repeating the same orders to those at oars. "Back to the *Revenge*. Row wit' the strength of many an' the courage of few!"

The blue current hovered just above them, a covering protecting them from the elements and the beast. Morrigan's feeding frenzy would not abate and the men fleeing the sinking galleon were never noticed. "It's blinding the Morrigan beast," Scala whispered, and Slade nodded.

While the blue current hid them, the men traversed the waters until finally reaching the *Revenge*.

Climbing aboard, most collapsed on the deck, too tired to speak. The pull had been fierce and had weakened the men in spite of fear's instinct for survival. Captain Phillips sat at a barrel and watched as Kathryn held steady the blue beam from her outstretched hands.

"It nearly kilt us, it did!"

"Aye, but ye've survived to live another day." Kathryn's voice was soft, peaceful. She glanced at John Phillips waiting for his response. As their eyes met, he wept.

"Yer back."

Kathryn nodded. Once all were safely on board, the blue current slowly disappeared. "Master Briggs, would you be so kind as to fetch Capt'n Phillips astrolabe and hourglass from his cabin? I've need of it to navigate this storm."

"Aye, Capt'n!" Briggs said, disappearing below deck.

Kathryn smirked and Phillips said nothing. He knew the men respected her once more. "Thank you, Capt'n...Kathryn," he fumbled, not knowing what title she would accept.

"Mellte Sosye, Chirurgeon, Capt'n...ye have your choice. But Kathryn is fine for now," she replied.

Briggs returned with the objects in hand and carefully set them at Kathryn's feet. She lifted the hourglass and peered into the glass, keenly observing the sand's never-ending drip. Then, picking up the astrolabe, she leveled it against a rail, following the water's crest toward the Morrigan. "This isn't over yet," she said, then glanced at John Phillips. "Ye'd best get prepared, and that means rest for the crew, feed them too."

"Aye," Gow stated, and Captain Phillips echoed the same. As Gow passed orders to the men still lying on the deck, Captain Phillips approached her.

"What does that tell you that I cannot see?" He asked

"It tells me that we have a great battle ahead of us. She…" Kathryn nodded to the skies and to Morrigan, "…isn't finished just yet. She wants us both, John. This will be harsh and one that I may not be able to stave off."

"I see," he replied. "And the men?"

"Many more will die, perhaps. That is difficult to see. But I know there are many souls that we cannot see with mortal eyes that will aid us, if we but call upon them."

"Ghosts?"

"Spirits of the dead," she replied. "Those that the Morrigan cannot reach. Those who have escaped her clenches. They await our request to join us in one final battle. We only need but call on them to help." She looked at his eyes and remembered how that gaze made her heart flux long ago. *Perhaps it will again, one day,* she thought pensively. "You, John, must go prepare yourself, as well."

"What of ye? Am I still Capt'n in yer eyes, as well?"

"You'll always be the Capt'n of the *Revenge*. As long as I sail aboard her, ye've command but I warn that ye do not make the same mistakes with me as ye've done before. I am not to be trifled with, John Phillips. I will walk beside you, a companion and trusted friend, but I will not be ordered about. Command the men but never command me again."

"Aye, Kathryn. And thank you." He turned to go then stopped, faced her, and kissed both of her hands. "Never forget, my beloved, who saved you from those who would have destroyed you. That was done in love, not by duty. Do not throw away he who loves you most." With that, Captain John Phillips walked from her and joined his men.

Kathryn smiled. "He understands now, as do I. With this, we can commence." She turned to face the sea and watched as the last vestiges of the Spanish galleon disappeared beneath the waves. Above, the Morrigan was nowhere to be seen, but Kathryn knew she remained, waiting. She rested her hands on the rails of her beloved *Revenge*. *Wait then, Morrigan. Wait until you're no more.* Kathryn smiled at the thought.

Wait indeed. And so would she.

Forty-Five

"A crimson dawn! It follows us."

"Aye…the Cutthroat's Omen." Scribbs swallowed hard, his mouth gone dry. "Ye know the sayin', 'Red sky at mornin', sailors take warnin'—"

"Red sky at night, sailor's delight." Kathryn cut in. "But we've none o' that, have we? Now back to work. This day will not likely end well for most o' us and ye need to be ready." The men gave one another a look then moved back to the guns. "And keep the powder dry," she added, though it was not her duty to oversee the powder monkeys or gunners, and those men were both.

"It won't matter the number of men we have onboard. This is not a battle anyone is familiar with. It'll be deadly no matter how many guns we man," she said, reading Phillips' thoughts as he stepped up next to her. She glanced at Scribbs and Dobs at their posts. "I just need time to think without their yammerin'."

"Kathryn."

She was lost in thought, eyes on the sea.

"Kathryn…lass. I know yer troubled, I can feel it. And I'll not tell ye how to fight this demon that comes for us, but I will tell ye this…Do not remember the battle but forget the blood that will be spilt this day."

She turned to face him. "Thank you, John. Thank you for rescuing me from an almost certain fate as a cottage girl."

"Oh-ho! So now it's a rescue and not a kidnappin'?"

"Thank you for teaching me how to survive amongst pirates…and at sea. Thank you for teaching me that love is more powerful than any dark force out there. Thank you for reminding me of who I am."

He stared into the pale blue pools of her eyes and noticed they had filled with tears, something he hadn't seen for a very long time. "I'm just grateful you are back and, in my life, again."

"I never left you, truly."

He pulled her close and she could feel the heat of his body through her rain-soaked clothing. The wind bit at them but she didn't notice as his lips met hers. Nothing existed in that instant. Only a pirate and his Celtic healer. The power of their love grew as strong as the kiss they shared in that moment.

Thunder rolled and a brilliant red flash touched the sea. The lightning bolt's crimson tip boiled the water where it landed. The jolt rocked the *Revenge*, forcing the couple apart.

"She's angry," Captain Phillips said.

"And she's coming for me," Kathryn replied.

"Nay," he shook his head and watched the water turn crimson, as well. "Nay, she comes for the both of us."

Kathryn sighed and watched the men begin to panic as each one caught sight of the red waters head. Gow moved forward and began to give orders. The men hopped to, some crossing themselves, other spat over the rails for luck. Slowly, the mist began to crawl from the boiling water toward the *Revenge.*

"Cutthroat's omen," someone yelled.

"It's happening again! To yer posts!" Gow shouted.

Across the deck, the crew's terrified bellows increased—sounds almost as fearful as the advancing mist. It was obvious the men would lose all hope before the battle even started. It's happened before at sea—men go mad with fear. This was Morrigan's plan, and Kathryn knew it. *Turn the men against themselves and Morrigan's won without a fight.* She groaned at the men's racket.

"The beast" and "heads will roll" and "We're goin' to die this time," their incessant panic escalated.

"Do something with your crew, Capt'n Phillips whilst I handle the mist Morrigan sends to greet us." Kathryn's calm demeanor caught him by surprise. Apparently, she wasn't too concerned about the mist or the crew dying because of it.

"Aren't you the least bit concerned? What about the crew? What about the beast we know lives in that vapor and… well, you know what happened last time, Kathryn."

"I am very aware of the beast. As I said before, you'd best tend to the crew and I'll tend to Morrigan's pet… unless, of course, you'd rather trade places and let me captain the crew again?"

He said nothing, turned to midship, and paced swiftly to face his men. Kathryn watched him move to his duty. *Who is really the captain, John Phillips? You or the Mellt Sosye?*

She smiled and turned her attention back to the sea.

Forty-Six

As the day progressed, the waters seemed to do the same, always churning, along with the sky that had advanced from vivid red to a bloody-crimson color as the sun dropped below the horizon. Even with night advancing, the skies remained their dark and blood-stained hue, marking something ominous that lay ahead deep in the Caribbean waters.

"It's an omen, it be," Skyrme said softly, polishing his pistol though he doubted it would be of any use. "We'd been better off leavin' the ship with th' others."

Slade kept his eyes on the tiny piece of wood he carved. There'd be no need for it either. Likely, they'd never play another game of trictrac again and gambling meant little to him, unless one could gamble for life. "Not bloody likely," Slade muttered under his breath.

"What er ye talkin' about? Of course, it's an omen, Slade. Just look up, man!" Skyrme's indignant reply went unnoticed.

"I wasn't talkin' to you."

"Oh. Well, then. That's different." Skyrme cleared his throat. "At least that's settled. A crimson omen it be, and we'd be better off—"

"The cutthroat's omen," Slade countered. "We're done-for, and best get ready to meet the devil himself, says I. Too late to leave now."

Skyrme stared at Slade wide-eyed, but he knew the pirate was right. They'd all likely die. Just how was the question.

Another brilliant flash of lightning touched down somewhere in the distance. The surf rolled and steam rose to form another black cloud. All life had silenced—no sound of birds or sea creatures calling to one another. The eerie quiet, broken only by lightning's crack and its following thunder, seemed more than the men could bear.

"Jangled nerves lead to wallowing seafarers," Gow stated the obvious. But no one responded. They all spoke the truth and each man knew it. Captain Phillips presence seemed to calm their hysterics but not their nerves. Now, all they could do was prepare to die.

Nutt held fast to the wheel, struggling to keep the *Revenge* on a straight course. The addition of Gow's strength at the wheel helped, but not much. "It rages and roars—the wild beast longs to leave its den."

"Needs to feed, it do."

Kathryn was nowhere to be found. It seemed critical to all of them that she remain topside, but then, who could say but that she'd brought the storm with her from the island. Few trusted her completely, and all feared her. Her absence spoke volumes.

She ran her fingers along the grainy planks, catching a fingernail on a loose trunnel and pulled. The wooden peg gave easily, and Kathryn was able to move the plank just enough to pull Mariel's book and satchel from behind. It had been a good hiding spot, even when she had been forced to leave the ship. The most valuable of her belongings were safe, provided the *Revenge* remained afloat. She nodded, satisfied that the objects remained intact and ready for her to call them to use. This was that time.

Carefully, so as not to snap the trunnel, she pushed on the plank and then set the peg back into place, ready to conceal her secrets for another day. Next, she snatched the Scarlet Seren, hanging from a small hook hidden underneath the mattress she used as a bed, and placed it gently around her neck. This, she would need later on. Finally, she pulled the Straif from its resting place in the corner of the room, then lit the single candle in the middle of her writing desk.

*"Bondye pwoteje nou kont Morrigan a epi ede
m mare l ak pwòp move aparèy li yo."*

The words tasted sweet in her mouth as she supplicated for power to do what she must in the Haitian Creole tongue.

"Deus nos protexa a todos (a tripulación, o barco e a min mesmo) do Morrigan e axúdame a ligala aos seus propios artificios malvados."

She concluded her next prayer in the ancient Galician language of her mothers and grandmothers. The candle's flame intensified then flickered. Satisfied, she blew it out.

"I am ready," she simply stated, and made her way up the causeway to the main deck.

No one spoke as she strode midship. Only the skies cried out on her approach. The *Mellt Sosyse* had arrived and presented herself to the sea, the storm…to the Morrigan.

Forty-Seven

"IMPRESSIVE ENTRANCE," CAPTAIN PHILLIPS SAID, tightening the baldric slung over his left shoulder.

Kathryn gave a slight smirk in response but kept her eyes forward. "Don't be rude, John."

"Those who now smile upon and embrace, would affront and stab each other, if manners did not interpose—"

"You quote Chesterfield."

"Ay," his smile more crooked than usual. "Though I be a pirate, I am still well-read, lass."

She looked at him askance. After all these years there was still more to learn about him. "I wonder what other gems ye keep hidden away, Capt'n Phillips."

"None that ye'd need be afraid of, dear Kathryn."

She shifted her weight and considered him. "Consider this, too many people spend time studying the properties of animals or herbs, but how much more important is to study those people with whom me must live…or die?"

"Oho! Wise words from Baltasar Gracian, ay? I see ye're studied as well."

"Only the writings of my grandmother, Mariel. She has a small library that Winne and I were privy to."

John Phillips hung his head. This would be difficult, but he had to tell her, and now was as good a time as any, given their circumstances. They were all likely to be dead by sundown anyway. He glanced at the sky and said a silent prayer for help.

"Kathryn, speaking of Winne. I've sommat to tell you. News, as it were." He cleared his throat hoping she'd somehow already known what he was about to say, but Kathryn remained still.

"Go on."

"Ye'd best hear this now, methinks. It'll be difficult but…"

She faced him. "Spit it out, John!"

"Winne was captured. Mary too, along with the silly Calico Jack. They'd been imprisoned in Jamaica, awaitin' hanging." He paused.

"And…?"

"Well, Rackham's dead. Hung with most o' his crew in Port Royal, including Earl, Dobbins, and Harwood… or so I heard. They say Jack still hangs above the port entrance as a warnin' to pirates."

"Mary?"

"No," he shook his head. "Mary's dead too, Kat. Claimed her belly at trial and it be true, according to me sources. Died givin' birth, apparently."

Kathryn shot him a look. "Continue."

"Mary was in prison when th' wee *cyw* was born."

Kathryn glanced at him. When anxious, Phillips' native Welsh would surface. Kathryn could tell he was edgy, indeed. He paused, waiting for her to take it all in. She stepped to the rails, and he followed.

"And what of Winne?"

Phillips paused, unable to speak the words. She turned to face him, her eyes calm and serene. "Never mind. I sense it. She hasn't crossed just yet but escaped the noose somehow." Kathryn turned back to look at the sea and skies and laughed. "Of course she did! You'll never get her, Morrigan, just like you'll never get me! Curse you, devil. Curse you and your foul sisters. I'll never join you."

The thunder that followed sent the mist hurling toward the *Revenge*. Behind it, a massive rogue wave. The moment Captain Phillips saw it, he ran to helm and yelled orders.

"Brace yerselves, men! Rogie's on approach!"

Kathryn gripped the rails and lifted her bandaged hand to touch the Seren that had turned as scarlet as the blood-stained skies.

"And so, it begins."

Beiridh caora dhubh uan geal.
A black ewe may have a white lamb.
~ ancient Gaelic proverb

PART THREE

Tyfónas

Forty-Eight

THE FIRST BLOOD-CURDLING SCREAM SOUNDED from the back of the ship. No one could see the deck, especially aft where another shriek cried out. The beast had boarded the *Revenge*. Just the smell alone was warning enough—one that the crew recognized immediately.

"Battle stations!" someone called out, but it was of no use. The beast stayed well-hidden within the vapor that continued its creep over the ship. Chaos ensued as men scrambled for safety, though where that would be was unknown. Only Kathryn knew what could be done…only the *Mellt Sosye* knew how to tame the beast.

Her voice sang out, a strange melodic pitch as an ancient Celtic spell formed from her throat, carrying the tones that broke through the dense vapor.

"Tha mi gad chumail air ais bhon fheadhainn a tha beò
Tha mi gad chumail air ais bhon fheadhainn a gheibh bàs
Bidh mi gad chumail air ais bho seo gu lèir."

The mist gnashed against her song but could not withstand the tones she used against it.

"What's she doin'?" Gow asked.

Slade crouched next to him. "She sings the Celts' *geis*. Watch, she'll do it three times, if done right and proper."

They kept their eyes on the mist but couldn't help but glance occasionally at Kathryn, whose voice carried as if a siren. Three times she sang the words and with each verse, another tone emitted, slicing the vapor as if with a sharp sword.

"She's cursin' it…spell-bindin', as it were. Look!"

Water hissed and twisted on itself as it fought against her song. Still, the mist would not withdraw. She tried a different pitch, singing in what sounded like two different voices. Again, the mist rose upright, like a cobra ready to strike.

"She's holdin' it," Gow said. "But it's not leavin'."

Slade just shook his head. "We're doomed. That's all there is to it," he replied and spat, then crossed himself. "Prepare to meet yer Maker, Bosun. We'll go together!"

Just then, Kathryn called out to the crew. "Fetch me Cook. I need him this instant."

In less than a heartbeat, Cook ran forward, cowering just behind her. "Cook's here, Miss Kathryn."

"Do you have any brass in the galley? Bowls are best."

"Aye."

"Fetch it and bring it to me…quickly!" she ordered.

Straightaway, Cook disappeared below deck and promptly returned carrying an ornately carved brass serving bowl. He held it out to her, still cowering from behind. "Swiped it from one o' those East India Trading ships. Methinks it's Indian writing there…"

"Perfect!" she said. "Now, hit it with something… anything! The ship's bell mallet works best." She sang tones again as he fetched the wooden mallet. "Hit it, Cook. Now!"

Cook tapped the side of the bowl with the mallet. A dull *ting* sounded. Kathryn snatched the objects from his hands and held the bowl flat on her palm, then struck the side of the bowl again and began to circle its rim with the mallet. A low, deep tone vibrated across the entire ship. She sang again, matching the tone of the brass bowl, then handed it back to Cook and nodded. He followed suit and likewise struck the side of the brass then circled the rim slowly. The same deep tone vibrated from the bowl.

"Don't stop, Cook. Keep the tone going." Then, to midship she cried out, "Someone strike the ship's bell… keep ringing it."

Captain Phillips stepped up beside her. "Kathryn…"

"Not now! Do we have chimes or crystal or any-thing that sings?"

"Bosun!" He looked at Gow. "I have goblets in my cabin."

"I'll get them, Capt'n," Gow said and disappeared.

"I can do this much." Captain Phillips reached for the brass bowl. Cook gladly gave it to him.

"Keep the tone steady, the mallet even and not too fast," she said.

"Aye." Then to his crew, "Check the gally for anything that might be useful as chimes or anything that—"

"Anything that hums or rings," Kathryn cut in. When Gow had returned with the crystal, she nodded and instructed the men how to run a finger around the rim to make it hum. Within moments, the ship was filled with the tones of ringing crystal and brass. "Now, hum yourselves!" she ordered.

"What tune do I—"

"Anything. A song from your childhood, a lullaby, shanties, or no song at all. Just hum!" she responded.

As the tones began to wash over the deck and fill the sails, the vapor seized. Gyrating, flinching, it recoiled and twisted on itself then pulled back into the sea. The creature within snarled and its foul smell followed. Again, the sea roiled, and its color turned crimson, but not with the blood of men. The crew of the *Revenge* remained alive, the few left there be.

<h1 style="text-align:center">Forty-Nine</h1>

"IT'LL BE BACK." SHE SPOKE softly then glanced at Captain Phillips. He stopped sounding the brass bowl and looked at the sea. "We only injured the beast and likely angered Morrigan. They'll be back and with a vengeance."

"What then? What do you foresee we do?" His voice remained steady although she could sense his fear.

Glancing at the crew, she shook her head. "I don't know...not yet."

"Then we kill the beast an' send th' Morrigan to the depths with it."

"It's not that simple John." Kathryn sighed. "She's powerful and angered, more powerful than we know. I saw this in the cave, in a vision. I know what she intends and how she'll do it."

Captain Phillips turned to face his men who stood stock still, waiting for orders. "Battle stations, *brwydrwr*."

"What's he sayin'?"

"Warrior. He calls us warriors!" Gow stood with cutlass in hand. "Hoy!" he shouted, raising it overhead.

Phillips nodded and continued, "This isn't over yet…not while we've fight in us." He raised his cutlass, as well.

Others soon followed, hoisting their blades in salute. "Hoy!" came the pirates' battle cry.

"We be pirates, and of the fiercest on these Caribbean Seas. Fight with yer might, yer soul, to the death if need be." Captain Phillips continued.

"Hoy!"

"Who's with me, mates? Let's battle this beasty— show 'er who owns these Caribbean waters…Ay!"

The men shouted again and set to preparations for another encounter with the beast. As if the Morrigan had heard their battle-cry, a heavy groan rolled from the clouds and the sea churned, but the mist remained at bay…for now.

"It's a fine speech, John, but these men can't beat her. You know this," Kathryn stated.

Phillips groaned. "You're so stubborn, Kathryn. Maybe there's hope…"

"Stop telling me everything you hate about me! Just stop it…please."

"Hate? You truly believe this?" John Phillips took a step back. "Your stubbornness is one of the things I love most about you! It will protect you—allow you to survive. But know this, Kat, it can also destroy you if not controlled."

"What are you talking about? I…I've always hated that about myself, my bull-headed, non-compromising, sheer stubbornness." Kathryn dropped her eyes and fought back tears. "My mum reminded me of this, frequently."

John placed his hands gently on her shoulders and pivoted her to face him. "My, beloved Kat…you are a force to be reconned with, but that force, the one out there…" He waved a hand at the sky, "…will kill us all unless we believe otherwise. You must believe…in yourself…believe in me."

She nodded, unable to choke back the lump that had taken its place in her throat. He was right and she had never been courageous enough to admit it before. This time, his words would save them all, if she could only believe in him the way his men did. Kathryn watched as the crew prepared themselves for what would surely be their last battle.

As if in agreement, the Seren began to glow. Reaching up to feel its warmth, her fingers touched the symbols etched in the stone and, suddenly, her eyes grew wide. For the first time ever, Kathryn comprehended its significance.

"The Seren! I know what the symbols mean!" She turned to the crew. "Get me the Straif. I need the Straif," she said, then frantically called to Briggs. "Please, get my Straif, Mister Briggs… there near the capstan."

Briggs ran across the deck to the capstan and retrieved the mahogany staff.

"The Madda Ooman was right." She looked up at Captain Phillips. "I know what to do, John. Why didn't Mariel tell me?"

By then, Briggs had returned with the Straif. Kathryn thanked him and instructed him to go back to the men and hum, once again. He darted aft, not wanting to be party to what she might ask of him next. Kathryn had been a good student and Wynn had taught her well. She learned the way of the blade quickly, but her temper and rogue mentality left both men a little nervous, and it showed, especially now.

Gently holding the Straif in one hand, she and ran her fingers across the etching. Placing her hand over the Seren, Kathryn began to sing. Slowly, the etched symbols began to glow a pale light that grew as her voice pitched. The Seren did likewise. She closed her eyes and listened to the light.

"What's she doin'," Gow whispered.

Slade shrugged and kept his eyes trained on her, as did the rest of the crew. Something was happening—something they'd never seen before and would likely never witness again.

Ethereal…magical…supernatural…and meant to defy evil.

She opened her eyes and looked at Captain Phillips. "You must be strong with this, John. Don't give in because she wants you…wants us both."

"Ay."

"The Straif speaks to me, ancient words that will bind the Morrigan. I hear them in the light. The pitch is too high for human ears and turns to light at that frequency, but I can hear it. I know what its sayin' and

I know what to do. We can bind her…send her to the depths, as it were."

"Ay, but she cannot die, lass," he shook his head. Beads of sweat covered his forehead and the locks of hair that rested there barely moved. "She's a goddess, eternal."

Kathryn smiled. "I know. But so are we. Our souls are eternal. Love is eternal. Those who are not seen are still with us for eternity—Mary, Calico Jack, the pirates who have died and dropped to Davy Jones' locker, my mum—all are eternal and their spirits, their energy is with us now. Can't you feel it?"

He said nothing afraid to admit he only felt rising panic.

Fifty

Terror spread across their faces and the pirates began to shiver. Heat rose in steam from the ocean even though it was dark. Nothing in that moment suggested a brisk bite to the air, so they shivered from something else. Fear most likely.

As if perceiving their dread, the water also shook, and a deep moan sounded from beyond the clouds. Rolling in thunder, a guttural whisper, the Morrigan issued her last warning:

Beware and do not cross—for the shadows of the night shall soon embrace you, and the cold hand of fate will guide you to the depths of hell where I will take your souls.

The goddess laughed and lightning cracked.

I perceive your thoughts Mellt Sosye, and yours as well, pirate. Know this—as the stars wane and the crimson dawn forgets your name, so to shall your breath be claimed in the silent depths of Hades!

She laughed again and the skies lit on fire as the water churned and boiled. Red skies and crimson waters poured beneath the *Revenge* while the men froze, terror overtaking them.

Kathryn lifted the Straif and held the Seren with the other hand. She closed her eyes and began to sing, deep, soulful tones that vibrated the very bones of anyone who heard her. The power of Seren and Straif illuminated symbols known only to the ancient Celts, and her words followed.

Ar n-Athair a tha air nèamh,
Gu naomhaichear d'ainm.
Thigeadh do rìoghachd.
Dèanar do thoil air an talamh, mar a nìthear air nèamh.

The skies groaned, this time with the wail of disturbance. Clouds turned blood-red and the waters greyed into deep purple.

"It's working," someone said.

Captain Phillips began to hum, his voice matching the tone of the brass bowl he now played. "Sing!" he ordered. Within moments, the crew had returned to playing tones on whatever object would make a sound, including their voices. Random tones in a dissonant pitch sounded from the pirates, some singing hymns, others humming whatever note they could muster, most sang sea shanties. The tones felt powerful, as did the men who made them.

Tabhair dhuinn an-diugh ar n-aran làitheil.
Agus maith dhuinn ar fiachan, mar a
mhaitheas sinne dar luchd-fiach.

Kathryn's song impacted the mist and Morrigan screeched, the song of a tortured beast. As she did so, the lightning took on its own form and sliced at the *Revenge*, but it could not reach the ship.

Agus na leig am buaireadh sinn, ach saor sinn o olc:
Oir is leatsa an rìoghachd, agus an
cumhachd, agus a' ghlòir, gu sìorraidh.

The *Mellt Sosye's* voice faded to silence, but the ship was not quiet. Whispers filled the ship and those aboard knew others had joined them. Kathryn opened her eyes and glanced behind her. Standing in pale shadows were the ghosts of her family's line, many generations back—her mum, Mary Read, Grandfather Whitefeather, Mari the Mystic, Winne, and her own grandmother Mariel. They formed a circle, holding hands, feet nearly three feet off the ground.

"Have you passed?" Kathryn asked Winne, who shook her head. Mariel did not, and Kathryn felt her throat tighten at understanding what that meant. "Winne, you are still with us?"

"Yes. We are here in spirit and soul to help you do this." Winne's voice sounded faint but sure.

"Look," another voice said, and the ghostly mystic pointed to where Kathryn had been shot. Kathryn looked down, lifting her shirt in time to see the bloody wound suddenly close. "You are healed in soul and body."

Thank you. The thought was heard and Mari smiled.

"Now, *Mellt Sosye*…bind her!" Winne and Mariel cried out together.

The command brought Kathryn's attention back to her foe—the Morrigan hovered overhead—from the clouds, her teeth gnashed, and blood dripped from each tine as she growled. Kathryn smirked and stepped onto the rails. Wynn, Dobs, and Skyrme ran up to hold her from tumbling into the ocean, though it wasn't necessary—Kathryn stood atop the rails of her own accord, supported by the unseen hands of those passed on.

"In the name of the Holy Ones, I command you to the depths of this sea, Morrigan."

The Morrigan's face twisted, fighting against the powerful *Mellt Sosye*. The sky turned black, and the lightning sliced but to no avail—Kathryn was too powerful. Slowly, bending to the sea, she touched the Straif to the water. It exploded, shattered sprays turned to diamond light, spreading out across the water to where the last remnants of the mist remained.

Morrigan screamed.

Covering their ears, the men dropped to their knees but somehow, continued to sing. Another scream sounded as Kathryn began to stir the water with the

Straif. Slowly at first, then building to a massive whirl-pool that began to spin, pulling everything within its reach into the center.

She then reached out to Captain Phillips. "Here is where you must be strong, my beloved." And to the men she cried out, "Do not fear, mates. Hold fast to your faith and continue your songs!"

In a final pitch, the light from the Straif and the tones from their voices met. The force of the vibration impaled the Morrigan, lobbing her from the skies and into the vortex spinning waters. The goddess cried out one last time before disappearing under the bubbling currents.

Fifty-One

"Is it over? Are we finished then?" Slade anxiously asked, and Kathryn shook her head.

"No. She's yet to be bound."

Several of the men, who had tied themselves to the rails with line, leaned over to see the black hole that spun not far from the *Revenge*.

"We're next! It'll pull us in too!" someone shouted midship, and a few of them scrambled to climb the masts, a better view to be had from up there.

Kathryn looked to Nutt, who gripped the wheel so tightly that his white knuckles could be seen from where she stood. As navigator, it was not his job to steer but there was no one else to do it, so he clung for dear life in hopes he could maneuver the *Revenge* out of danger. Not likely.

"Mister Nutt," she shouted when she'd caught his attention. "Where are we now? What are these waters?"

"The Triangle—twixt Bermuda Isle, the New Colonies and Leeward Isles," he shouted back.

Kathryn stared at the vortex. Captain Phillips watched, waiting for some suggestion as to what might happen next. "What say ye, lass. I've a ship to save if ye've nothin' else."

She regarded him for a moment before she spoke. "The Morrigan must be bound. The vortex cannot hold her as it is. I fear it may take the ship." She motioned to the sea. "Are you ready?"

He studied the water and knew there was little else they could do. Morrigan had been chasing him for nearly three years. Perhaps she had finally caught up with him. "Ay," he said and turned to face his men. "Ready yerselves mates, we've a devil to keep to the sea. Hold tight to whatsoever ye can find and follow all orders."

Another crack of lightning flashed, and the wind began to howl. Kathryn noticed it sounded much like the Morrigan's wail and readied herself to bind the goddess-devil forever in the sea. Lifting her arms overhead, she called out to the lightning.

Giùlain ar n-ùrnaighean suas gu rìgh-chathair
Dhè, gun tig tròcair an Tighearna gu luath, agus
gun dèan i greim air a' bhiast, an nathair o shean,
am Morrigan agus a deamhain, ga tilgeadh ann
an slabhraidhean anns an dubh-aigein, gus nach
bi i nas fhaide air a mhealladh. anama nam beo.

Wide-eyed, Gow said aloud what every man thought. "She's speakin' Galician. The language o' the

Scots." He turned to Captain Phillips who nodded in agreement. "When'd she learn Galician?"

Captain Phillips shrugged, "I suppose she's always known it, mate. We just didn't know it."

Kathryn repeated the holy words, shifting the canonical prayer into almost a chant, and as she did so, the lightning flashed even brighter.

*Thig tròcair an Tighearna gu luath, agus glacaidh
i a' bhèist, an nathair o shean, am Morrigan agus
a deamhain, ga tilgeadh ann an slabhraidhean
anns an dubh-aigein gu bràth agus gu sìorraidh.*

As she spoke the last, bolts of light flashed from the sky to the vortex and again from Kathryn hands, forming a triangle of white-hot light. The *Mellt Sosye* illuminated and whispers from the spirits who joined her grew brighter, as well. The *Revenge* and her crew were completely bathed in light, and several of the men covered their eyes trying to shut out its brilliance, but it couldn't be done. A few cried out in pain, others cowered, preparing themselves for death. Only Kathryn and her beloved pirate captain remained upright, steadfast, and focused.

Another crack and a shattering ripple spread out from Kathryn's hands to the sea and the sky, again a perfect triangle.

"Mother, maiden, crone. The Triskele. I am the fourth sister and will not join you. But I alone have the power to bind you, Morrigan, my evil sister." The water surged as she spoke and those who dared the light to peek at the vortex saw the Goddess' face, twisted and desecrated.

"Do it," Captain Phillips stated.

Kathryn opened her eyes and stared at the face swallowed in the vortex and gave one last command as the *Mellt Sosye*—the fourth sister of the Morrigan.

"I bind you to the depths of these waters, never to surface, for all eternity. So be it!"

With her final command, she pitched the Straif into the center of the vortex. And then…Kathryn collapsed.

PART FOUR

Finis est Principium

Fifty-Two

"It shall ever be known as 'The Devil's Triangle'," Captain Phillips announced. "Those who sail here do so at their own risk."

The pirates nodded and muttered amongst themselves.

"But what of Bermuda Isle. It's a good tradin' port, an' we…" Dobs began but Captain Phillips cut him off.

"We'd best stay clear o' these waters. She's not completely gone, no! The devil Morrigan is banished, bound, as it were an' stays under the crest of the currents for all eternity."

Slade cleared his throat, but Capt'n…if the Morrigan be down there…" he nodded to the froth where the vortex had been. "…then what will be of the ships that route through here for tradin'?"

"I cannot say, Mister Slade. But yer question is a good one. Most likely, she'll wreak havoc on any passersby, methinks."

"Poor devils. They'll never know what happened to 'em," Slade replied, shaking his head.

Captain Phillips motioned to Skyrme. "She needs sommat to drink."

Skyrme jumped to and, rubbing his eyes as he scurried, fetched a mug for Kathryn. The captain took it from his outstretched hand and offered it to Kathryn, who sat, leaning against his broad chest. When she had taken a few sips, she lifted the mug in salute.

"I drink to my crewmates and loyal friends. This could not have been done without every one of ye. And your captain is correct, the Morrigan still thrives below the water's depths. She's bound by three, to be certain, but no one can know what mayhem she'll inflict in this Devil's Triangle." Kathryn took another sip and glanced up at the captain, who smoothed her hair from her face. "John, we're still in danger here. We'd best set sail quickly and leave this place."

"Ay," he agreed. "Your Straif?"

"It's served its purpose and will continue to keep her pinned below. The symbols on its surface are powerful and its light overpowers Morrigan's darkness. This was its intent when created. Pedro understood this."

Captain Phillips sighed. "Ah, Pedro. Would that he'd chosen a different course."

"Aye, but it was his to make and likely, he knew what would happen." She smiled. "I saw him with us on deck when Morrigan was bound. He's in spirit, now."

"Mayhaps his purpose then, too?"

"Aye," she nodded. "They are all gone now, and we are on our own. Pick a course that takes use north, John…to Nova Scotia, methinks."

Captain Phillips gave her a puzzled look but knew better than to challenge her. Calling new orders to his men, they set the sails and redirected the ship over the shifting waters that would always be known as the Bermuda Triangle.

"Take our bearings to Nova Scotia, Mister Nutt," the captain shouted, and Nutt responded. Gow followed suit, hustling the few men that remained on deck to their duties. Though the sea was calm, the water below the surface remained black, angry, and churned. Except for the bubbly froth that hid the home of the devil's daughter, no one would ever know what had happened there.

As the hull cut a line through the foam, the wind filled the sails, and the men began to whistle. Hope had returned to the *Revenge*—a new hope that better fortunes might be found in a place known as Nova Scotia.

Fifty-Three

"Bᴜᴛ ᴡʜʏ ɴᴏʀᴛʜ, ʟᴀss? Wʜʏ not back to the Caribbean and the waters we know so well. Nova Scotia holds little for pirates."

Kathryn pulled three pieces of leather from the hiding place in her quarters. "*This*…is the reason we must go north, and the reason I asked you to speak privately with me in my quarters."

Phillips looked around the room, as if someone were hiding in the shadows. But he saw no one. He shook his head. "Are those what I think they be?"

"Aye," she said, untying the cord that held each rolled up tightly. Placing the first on a table, she flattened it out and pointed. "This piece, I cut from Cameat's thigh. You remember him, don't you?"

Captain Phillips nodded and swallowed hard. "You mean to tell me that this is a map cut from Father Debaraz's flesh?"

"Oh, *pffffft!*" She waved a hand in the air. "He was but a crazed lunatic kept too long in irons. He lost his mind, John. Barely winced when I cut the marking out of his leg."

Phillips grimaced. "He didn't put up a fight?"

"Oho! Not even a whimper." She pulled the cord from the second rolled up leather. "This one is very interesting. A little delicate but very critical to our plan."

The skin was soft and much more pliable than the first. She laid it flat, positioning it alongside the first. Lines tattooed in both skins crossed the length of the cuts. He glanced at her and grimaced.

"Cut from a corpse." His eyes widened as she spoke. "Oh, don't be so delicate, John. She never felt it and certainly won't miss it, methinks. The rest of her feeds the fish, so we're lucky I snatched it off of her rotting flesh before it was lost forever." Laying the third below the others, she tapped the skin excitedly. "Now, look at this one."

"Kathryn!" Captain Phillips protested, but she ignored him.

"Look here," she said, pushing the edges against one another. "All of the lines match up on all three pieces. They fit together perfectly."

Captain Phillips noticed the excitement in her voice. Something unusual about the markings stood out—he recognized their pattern but could not place where he'd seen it before.

"What am I lookin' at, lass?"

"Come now, John. Can you not tell what this is?"

"Well," he turned his head as if that would clarify exactly what he viewed. "...could be a map?"

"Aye!" Kathryn nearly leapt. Clutching at his neck, she pulled him to her and kissed him. "A map indeed… and not just any map, John. This map will change our lives! But there is one section missing…here. Do you see it?" She did not wait for his answer. "Give me your arm."

He held out his arm and she pushed up the fabric of his sleeve to expose the Lichtenberg Figures still patterned over his tanned skin. Aligning her own, she pressed her forearm against his and the patterns merged—another set of lines.

Phillips gasped. "How could this be?"

"Look here," she said and drew both of their arms to the leathery maps spread out flat. "See, this is the last. We…you and I…a part of the plan. That is why no one could find it before."

"Find what, Kathryn? Are you suggesting this is…"

"Aye! A treasure map. And these are the marking that will lead us to it."

His eyes widened. "They're ley lines! That's how I recognized them!" She smiled and watched as his eyes grew wide. "…that lead to Nova Scotia."

She grinned and nodded. "Now you understand, aye?"

Within moments, the ship had sailed out of the troubled waters of the Bermuda Triangle and was well on its way north. Should the winds stay with the sails, they would made landfall in a week. While neither Kathryn nor Captain Phillips had revealed their plan or the destination, the crew sensed something promising in the venture. No one asked questions. No one cared much about why the pirates traveled their current course. They were alive and well on their way to a new destination and a new adventure.

Perhaps treasure is personal and unique to every man. Perhaps, each man (and woman) defines their own success and the treasure they hold dearest. This seemed to be true of the crew, their captain, and the Celtic healer that sailed aboard the pirate ship, *Revenge*.

PART FIVE

Vita Perpetua

Fifty-Four

"Decreed forthwith this day, in the year of our Lord, seventeen twenty-four, and upheld before this magistrate who doth represent His Majesty, King George the First, upon these shores of the province of Acadia…"

Her azure eyes scanned the crowd gathered at the base of the moss-covered berm, the curious steadily increasing in numbers. Only a few wiped their faces as they glanced briefly in her direction. There were those who feared her and looked upon her demise as a gift of providence. She smiled softly in response to the few who wept, the only act of kindness she would receive this day.

"…and hereto resolving matters of crimes committed against England, Scotland and Spain, as well as the good people of this community…"

She glanced to her right and caught his regal features falter momentarily as he studied the ocean not far from where they stood together.

"…it is hereby declared that the lady, Kathryn McCauley Phillips be guilty of witchcraft and piracy…"

His emerald gaze darted from the turquoise water and bore into the magistrate as he spoke her name. The Lord Magistrate's voice rang out blasphemy, speaking her name thus, pronouncing each syllable with such callousness. Could he but free himself from the bonds tethering his hands together in front of his body, he would lash out and carve the tongue from the man's throat.

"John," she whispered, and his eyes left the pious Lord who continued his pontifications, unaware of the pirate's plans to murder him. Her eyes met his and the intertwining of colors, his emerald with her azure blue, created a blending of hues to match the waters of their beloved Caribbean.

"John Phillips, also known as John Phillips Buchanon, for the crimes of piracy, murder, thievery, and debauchery…"

His focus snapped back to the pompous magistrate decorated in ribbons of authority and a tattered grey wig. One bloated hand gripped a long silver oar, the symbol of appointed nautical authority, although there was little doubt that this fool had ever been anything but a landlubber. The other hand was wrought with tremors, the result of a needed nip on the bottle most likely hidden in a desk drawer somewhere. The rolled piece of parchment from which he read rattled with his trembling, silenced only by the crash of the waves where freedom lay just out of reach.

"…the penalty for each of ye…"

Both prisoners stared directly at the man with the oar and prepared for his declaration.

"…is death by hanging until dead, dead, dead."

Kathryn closed her eyes against the sentence as a shriveled man stepped forward, the only other person standing upon the hastily erected platform. He pulled a large cross from beneath his tunic and began hissing last rites as he circled them across the unsteady planks, casting holy water at their feet.

"…and to ensure that the devil doth not unleash his daughter upon this earth once again, an additional sentence of death by fire be declared upon Kathryn McCauley Phillips."

"No!" A cry from the back of the small crowd wailed, the raspy alto familiar to Kathryn.

"Silence! We have many witnesses who attest to her fiendish deeds, all bespeak of witchcraft and sorcery," the magistrate's comments directed to an unseen objector intermingled within the gathered onlookers. He scanned the crowd but could not identify the source.

Kathryn's eyes fixed on the cloaked figure in the back.

Be still cousin! They cannot take me, nor can they hinder the Gift given to us. Protect that which is most precious by holding your tongue and allow what will be.

The thought floated from her heart and Kathryn watched blonde curls spill from beneath the cloak chaperon as the woman's head nodded unwillingly. She shifted something held under the protection of the long black cape covering her identity as well as her infant charge. Kathryn knew her cousin had received the message.

As the executioner placed the hood, she glanced at John. His would be the last face she would see in this moment…and the first in the next. His returned gaze was implicit that he understood.

"Have faith, my love," she whispered.

A rope placed hastily around both of their necks was tightened to where the knot sat against their nape, and within moments, the latch had been released. Gasps followed from the audience, and some turned their faces. A hanging was never pleasant, although often entertaining.

Just then, the incendiary stepped forward with a torch, ready to ignite the woman's skirts but a voiced called out, "Wait!"

"Who interjects? This is government business, and the witch must be burned, as is custom!"

The voice called out again. "No! Stop. That is not the witch!"

Murmuring from the crowd drowned out what was said next, but an order to remove the hoods to verify death was given. As the executioner stepped forward, the crowd pressed in for a better look. This day had brought a truly eventful hanging!

Her hood was removed, and brilliant coppery hair cascaded to the woman's shoulders. Taking her by the scalp, the executioner lifted her head to reveal a face that did not belong to Kathryn.

"Quickly! The other!" the Magistrate ordered.

And as the hood was pulled from the man, the cropped blonde hair revealed it was not the pirate they'd hung.

Audible gasps came from the audience as witnesses realized the bodies did not belong to Kathryn McCauley or John Phillips.

"Where are they? What happened to the bodies?" The Magistrate's face turned beet-red and his trembling into convulsive amblings, running back and forth in front of the hangman's platform, as if doing so would help him find answers.

No one knew the identity of the bodies hanging from the nooses. No one recognized their puffy, blue faces. No one noticed the sunset as it changed color or the three cloaked persons that dashed away from the crowd toward the sea.

As they neared the ley line that would take them to the waiting ship, Winne cast back her hood and laughed. She handed the baby in her arms to its mother, who began to hum a familiar Celtic lullaby. In the distance, a tall brigantine signaled.

"Seth has readied the ship and awaits us, as planned."

As the portal revealed itself, they stepped onto the ley line and were never seen again.

NON-EST FINIS
So it is written…
So it is done.

Those who bothered to watch from the shore saw it. It lasted barely a breath but the flash of green light over the horizon materialized, just for an instant. And as it did, the *Revenge* disappeared, along with the light.

Only two remained long enough to make certain the ship had made it safely into the unknown. He dropped the tricorn onto his head and took her by an arm. "Come Alex."

"*Et sic scriptum est… sic factum est,*" were her only words, and nobody heard them. But it didn't matter. He understood. Turning from the sea's horizon, they walked away, smiling.

And so it was written…so it is done.

Midnight Omen

The Déjà vu Chronicles (book 1)

"What J. K. Rowling did for wizards, and Stephenie Meyer did for vampires, Marti Melville has done for pirates" (Forbes Magazine Online, 2011)

https://doceblantstore.com/collections/paranormal-horror

Silver Moon

The Déjà vu Chronicles (book 2)

A paranormal, historical adventure based on the life of a real pirate from the 18th century Caribbean.

https://doceblantstore.com/collections/paranormal-horror

Onyx Rising
The Déjà vu Chronicles (book 3)

The power of a witch, the cunning of a pirate!

https://doceblantstore.com/
collections/paranormal-horror